BLUE MOON

Books by John Leslie

Blood on the Keys
Bounty Hunter Blues
Killer in Paradise
Damaged Goods
Havana Hustle

Gideon Lowry Mysteries:

Killing Me Softly
Night and Day
Love for Sale
Blue Moon

Published by POCKET BOOKS

BLUE MOON

A Gideon Lowry Mystery

JOHN LESLIE

POCKET BOOKS

New York London Toronto Sydney Tokyo Singapore

POCKET BOOKS, a division of Simon & Schuster Inc.
1230 Avenue of the Americas, New York, NY 10020

ISBN: 0-671-53514-5

First Pocket Books hardcover printing September 1998

10 9 8 7 6 5 4 3 2 1

POCKET and colophon are registered trademarks of
Simon & Schuster Inc.

Printed in the U.S.A.

For Barbara,
who helped hatch the plot at dinner
one long-ago night in Missoula

◇

"Location, location, location. You've heard that before, haven't you, Bud?"

Staring above Frank Pappagallo's inquisitive gaze, I take in the framed photographs on the wall above his head—all the transformations this establishment has undergone over the years—and recognize them all. *Welcome to the Blue Moon, Key West's only five-star restaurant.* So the menu reads.

"Don't patronize me, Frank," I say. "I wasn't born yesterday." For the price of the food, the company could be more appetizing, I think. On the other hand, I'm not paying. On still another hand, I'm too old to have to listen to such crap.

"And I don't give a damn about real estate slogans," I continue, warming a bit to my own tirade. "I've lived in this town all my life. So what if somebody wants to pay me five times what the place is worth and ten, maybe twenty times what I paid for it God knows how many years ago. It's my home. I live there. What am I going to do, move every time some new pip-squeak with a fat wallet comes to town and decides this is it? The next hot spot. Location, location, location. They might as well hang a sign outside Key West changing its name to Location. How many times have you seen this place change, anyway?"

"Don't get sore, Bud."

Bud. My high school nickname. Hardly anyone from the old days calls me Gideon any longer. . . .

"Who's getting sore? I'm sixty years old, trying to live out my life and keep a little business going."

"I want you to do that, Bud. Everybody wants you to do that. But why in the middle of Duval Street?"

"Because it's my home, Frank. My home. Can't you understand that. I live here. I feel something for it. It's not just a place to do business. My life's here."

Frank sighs. "For half a million dollars I could take my life someplace else."

"That's the difference between you and me, Frank."

"I know it. And by the way, it isn't a new pip-squeak."

"Yeah, who the hell is it?"

"Fred Pacey's involved."

"Pacey's moving uptown? I thought he was happy making millions downtown."

I can see that Frank's smile is forced. He is uncomfortable. "Location. A higher-class neighborhood. Speaking of high-class neighborhoods, how do you like your dinner?"

"Twice-cooked pork. What's wrong, they couldn't get it right the first time?"

Now Frank looks hurt.

"I'm kidding, Frank. Seriously, I'm happy for Gaby. I've known her for a long time. When she first opened, it was rice and beans and fried plantains. Now look at the place. Starched linen. Thirty-dollar bottles of wine. And food I can't even pronounce."

"Three blocks from where you live, Bud. When she first opened, she was paying a couple hundred dollars a month rent. Now it's five thousand. You don't make that kind of money serving rice and beans. Gabriella!"

"Hi, Frank. Look who you dragged in. Bud, it's been a long time. How have you been?" Gaby is tall, slender, with minty green eyes that survey me warmly. An old friend. She is wearing a simple dark blue dress with thin straps, her dark hair curling just above her bare shoulders.

"No complaints. We were just talking about the old days, Gaby, when you first started in the restaurant business."

Gaby smiles happily, putting a hand on my shoulder. "You were a regular." Her expression is open, honest. Never anything spoiled about Gaby, just as I remember her from so many years ago when we were close. She seems unchanged.

"I could afford to be," I say. "Now I've got to wait for somebody with deep pockets like Frank here to bring me in. He's trying to get me to sell my place."

"Don't make any deals until you've had dessert. Try the crazy *flan borracho*. It's flavored with Cointreau. It's on me. I've got to run. Enjoy your meal."

"She's something. You used to go out with her, didn't you, Bud?"

"Briefly. A long time ago."

"You old dog. I hear she's getting married."

"Who to?"

"Don't know. She's a looker though, isn't she, Bud? How old you think she is?"

3

"Mid-thirties. Somewhere in there."

"Her first, isn't it?"

"What?"

"Marriage."

"As far as I know."

"She's worked hard. Nose to the grindstone the last ten years or so to put this together."

I nod idly, lost in thought about Gaby. Remembering the way her body felt when she would come over some mornings after I'd played a late club date and, fresh from a shower, slide into bed with me.

"Anyway, Bud, you'll think about it?"

"Did Pacey put you on me, Frank? Is that what this is all about?"

"Please, Bud. You know me better than that. We go back, you and me. I wouldn't do that. I'm just the messenger passing along the word I hear on the street."

"That's good of you, Frank. The word according to Fred Pacey."

"He's buying up your block, Bud."

"For what? More T-shirt shops?"

"A mall. Upscale."

"You don't say."

Frank shrugs. I know he is terribly uncomfortable, that he isn't going to push this. "Bud, how about dessert?"

"I don't drink."

Frank laughs, relieved. "Gaby's got ice cream. Plain old vanilla."

"You know my weaknesses."

"He's already got the Cuban grocery store next to you."

"What?"

"Pacey. He's buying the little *groceria* next door to you."

A twinge of pain stabs my side. "I'll take the vanilla ice cream," I say.

Frank smiles weakly. "I'm sorry."

"Hey, it's only a neighborhood. What's the price?"

"I hear three-seventy-five."

"A steal."

"You're getting the idea."

"I don't think so, Frank. Like you say, I'm an old dog. Too old for these new ideas."

"You thinking at all about retirement, Bud?"

"What's to retire from? Nobody's beating the door down to hire a private detective these days. We're a dying breed. The Edsel of occupations."

"That's funny, Bud."

"I wish I could laugh with you."

"So you're sixty years old. Not a lot of work. But you've got some money saved and a house that's a gold mine. Why not take the money, get yourself off Duval Street, move in to some quiet noncommercial neighborhood. What's the sense of hanging on there? I don't see how you sleep at night, the traffic and noise all hours."

"I sleep just fine. Nothing on my conscience."

"You're a pistol, Bud."

"Drink your dessert, Frank. I enjoyed the meal but this discussion's given me a pain in my side. You don't mind, I think I'll take a powder, walk home and get my last view of Duval Street before the sidewalks get paved with gold and I can't afford to walk on them anymore."

◇

Three hundred and seventy-five thousand dollars. A lot of money for a grocery store no bigger than a small gas station, a mom-and-pop outfit selling Cuban mix sandwiches in waxed paper, a few condiments and canned goods, icy cold beer and soda, and the best espresso coffee in town. Locals come all day for a hit of *buche* or a *con leche* to jump-start the morning or provide a little pick-me-up during the day. The place is legendary. And now, apparently, it's closing. Selling out to make room for another mall. Upscale, according to Frank Pappagallo, a lawyer, my lawyer, who in the last few years has begun to specialize in real estate law. Frank seems to know when something is going to sell before the owner even knows his place is on the market.

Sad about Mom and Pop. But understandable, I suppose. Who can blame them? They're an elderly Cuban couple who run the place, with a little help from a couple of their grown kids. Over a quarter of a million dol-

lars for a wooden shack with old wooden floors that are
termite-eaten, the varnish long gone, the boards worn
smooth under the constant tread of feet day in and day
out for more years than I care to remember.

Frank. *Just the messenger,* he said. The pain in my
side is like the dull, crippling sickness following a sudden blow to the groin. Spreading in waves somewhere
below the rib cage and around to my lower back. A hell
of a thing to eat a meal like that and feel like this afterward, I think.

Just the messenger. Maybe he is right. What the hell
am I hanging on to here, anyway? Get out before I'm
squeezed out. While I still have some leverage. Buy a
little bungalow on the other side of town, out of sight of
the commercial strip this street has become, and forget
about it. Let Pacey have it. What is this absurd attach-
ment to Duval Street, anyway?

At the corner is a traffic light, and I pause in my
walk, leaning into the pain in my side with my fore-
arm, as if I can somehow force it into a more manage-
able place, or dispel it altogether. It doesn't seem like
indigestion, but maybe a couple of antacid tablets will
do the trick. Fizz, fizz.

Past the juice bar, the art gallery, the ice cream parlor,
and the all-night convenience store that gets held up
regularly by crack addicts. None of this was here five
years ago. And most likely none of it will be here five
years to come.

And neither will I if Fred Pacey has his way. There
is a light on inside, barely illuminating the windows
with their crumbling gold lettering advertising the
Lowry Detective Agency, but it is a welcome relief to
step up on the porch and, after unlocking the front

door, go inside and close the door on the world for a moment. Alone.

Sitting down in the swivel chair behind my desk, I find the antacid tablets in the top drawer and gulp a couple of them, then lean back in the chair, putting my feet on top of the desk. Staring at the ceiling. There is the click of paws on the wood floor as my tomcat comes in from the kitchen to check out my arrival. At least twenty years old, he is blind now in one eye and measures each move before he makes it. I watch as he slowly rubs a paw over his good eye, then pulls himself gingerly into the open lower desk drawer where he now spends so much of his time, also withdrawn from the world.

Nearly thirty years in this house, twenty of them with a cat who showed up uninvited on the back step one day and never left; a relationship that surprisingly has lasted, longer than any of my three marriages.

The pain is spreading now like hot lava across my abdomen. Something is wrong. A couple of deep breaths, waiting, I now know futilely, for the antacids to kick in. During my life I've been spared illness. This kind of pain is foreign and therefore, perhaps, all the more forbidding.

Easing my feet off the desk, I realize that I'm moving much like the cat, staring now at the phone as I consider calling a doctor. Few of the local doctors are left, except for Doc Russell, who is ten years older than I and still practicing. Whenever I have needed some modest medication over the years, he has providently filled a prescription for it without making a big deal out of my reluctance to come to the office. I look up his home phone number. It is ten-thirty, and I am sure that

I will wake him with a call at this hour. But he answers on the first ring.

"Bud, what's wrong?"

There is a certain huskiness to his voice and a faint slur in his speech. I wonder if he has been drinking and remember that Russell has a reputation for enjoying his cocktails, and for being quick with the knife.

"Doc, I've got a strange pain that seems to be getting worse."

"Where is it?"

I tell him.

He asks a couple more questions about my activities in the past twenty-four hours, punctuating each of my responses with an ominous *hmmm* before asking if I still have my appendix.

"No, you took it out when I was a teenager. Over forty years ago."

"Oh, I forgot."

"I would have forgot, too, except I've still got the scar to prove it."

Doc Russell chuckles. I find myself actually wincing aloud with pain. "Bud, you got a choice. Go to the hospital, or I'll come over and check you out and you may still have to go to the hospital."

"How serious is it?"

"I can't make a diagnosis over the phone." Russell sounds peeved.

"Well, then maybe you ought to come over."

The doc sighs. Then, I hear him in a muffled voice say something to his wife. When he comes back to me, he says, "Bud, I got to be the last MD in the country who will make a house call. And at damn near eleven o'clock at night, no less."

"At your age you don't need sleep."

9

"I'll be there in fifteen minutes."

I hang up. The pain has now taken on roller-coaster proportions. My skin is clammy with sweat. Never having been in the grip of any serious illness before, I begin to envision the end. But half an hour later, Doc Russell laughs, and says, "Bud, you got colitis. Get off the spicy foods. I'm going to put you on a diet, and in a week you'll be good as new."

3

◇

I hope it wasn't something you ate, Bud." Gaby stands in my office the next morning, where I am stretched out on the old leather sofa. It has been a long night. The pain lasted into the early hours, and it was after three in the morning before I finally got any sleep.

"What are you doing here?"

"I came in when I heard that you were sick."

"Who told you I was sick?"

"Frank called me."

"How did he know?"

"You know Frank. He's a lawyer." Gaby smiles. "He hears everything. Sometimes before it even happens."

My lawyer. When I needed one. Fortunately, like doctors, that has not been often. Frank and I were born and raised in Key West. Friends, I suppose. Though, like he had last evening, he could get on my nerves at times.

"I've got to go on a diet. No more spicy foods. Cut out the coffee. First the alcohol goes. Then caffeine."

"It could be worse."

"Sure. I could take a vow of celibacy." Memories of Gaby from a different time play across my brain like a melody from some distant tune.

Gaby smiles, but looks away.

"I hear you're getting married," I say.

"Frank told you that?"

"Who else?"

"I've been meaning to talk to you for a while, Bud. In fact, when you're feeling better, I'd like for you to come and see me."

"Sure. Where you living now?"

"Up the Keys. On Sugarloaf."

"Nice." It was the country. Twenty miles out of Key West.

"It's quiet. After working in the restaurant late every night, it's a relief to get out there."

"You don't mind the drive?"

"No, it's a good transition."

I can't imagine it. Just the prospect of leaving Duval Street seems unsettling. The bell on the front door tinkles, and Frank comes in with a couple of carryout containers of coffee. It smells good. "I can't drink that stuff," I tell Frank.

"Sorry. I didn't know."

"I didn't either until last night. I've just been lamenting my new regimen with Gaby."

She smiles, bends down, and kisses my cheek. Her face is cool next to mine. "I've got to go," she says. "I meant it about coming up, though."

"Maybe tomorrow."

"Good. I'll keep the morning open." She turns toward the door. "Why don't you come for lunch?"

"Sure."

"Take care, Frank," Gaby says.

"Here, have a coffee," Frank tells her. "Get rid of the temptation."

Gaby laughs, takes the offered cup, and leaves.

Frank's dark hair, which I know he colors, is slicked down and still wet. He looks as if he has just recently gotten up. He also looks like he has a hangover. "Bud, what is this?"

"I suppose, Frank, what it is is age. Things start breaking down."

Frank shuffles around uncomfortably, blowing on the surface of his coffee. "How's your insurance, Bud?"

"What do you mean, how is it? What are you talking about, Frank?"

"I mean you're covered, aren't you?"

"Frank, I've got colitis, not cancer. Don't write me off yet."

"I'm just thinking ahead. If you ever had to go into the hospital, you've got plenty of coverage. That's all."

"I've got insurance, Frank."

"What's your deductible?"

"Frank, you're a pain in the ass sometimes. I don't know what it is. Three grand, five. I don't remember."

"That's high. Maybe you ought to reduce it."

"Then my premiums go up."

Frank takes a sip of his coffee, then puts the cup down on my desk. "Well," he says, "if anything happens you've got the house."

"Frank, we had this discussion last night. I'm not in the mood for it now. If Fred Pacey put you up to this, you've got a lot to answer for."

Frank holds his hands out as if he's pushing something away from him. "Believe me, Bud. As your lawyer, I'm only looking out for your interests."

"That's big of you, Frank. Don't do me any favors."

The familiar hurt look comes over Frank's face. "Sure, Bud. I'm not pressing it. Anything I can get for you?"

"Yeah, a couple of scrambled eggs and some grits. That's bland enough."

"I'll go over to the drugstore and pick it up. After, we can play a couple hands of pinochle."

I haven't played pinochle since my first marriage, to Peggy, when we played with another couple every week. Over thirty years ago.

When Frank returns with the food, I eat half of it, then let him talk me into the card game. We play at opposite sides of the desk, Frank bantering while the cards are dealt. After an hour, I call a halt.

"Get out of here now," I tell Frank. "I don't need a nursemaid. I'm fine."

"All right, Bud. But call if you do need anything."

"I'll call when I need a lawyer."

Frank laughs nervously, and limps out the door.

4

◇

At eleven-thirty I go next door to the *groceria* and get a Cuban toast with cheese melted on it, and sublimate my desire for a *con leche* with a cold ginger ale. Pop is working the espresso machine, and I can see Mom making sandwiches beyond the opening in the wall to the tiny kitchen.

"Bud, someone tell me you been sick?" Pop says. He is a small man with thick salt-and-pepper hair combed straight back, always immaculate in a white shirt that looks as if it has just been washed and ironed.

"Nothing serious. Just got to change my eating habits."

Pop smiles and says something I don't hear against the roar of the espresso machine as he froths milk in a silver pitcher for a *con leche* for someone else. From the kitchen Mom pokes her head out the window and gives me a friendly wave.

When he puts the toasted cheese in its wax paper on

the counter beside the *con leche*, I tell him I have heard he is selling the business.

Pop looks at me gravely. "Bud, what can I do? They come in here. They offer money, cash money, like I don't see ever before."

"Pop, they're offering you half of what this place is worth."

He lays his delicate hands on the counter. "Is a lotta money, Bud." Pop looks around the store, his business, as if taking an inventory and disbelieving what he finds. A few cans of black beans, some bags of rice. Staples. The cold colas and beer. I can see it in his eyes: Why would anybody want to pay that much money for this?

"I don't know, Bud."

"Think about it. You haven't signed anything yet, have you?"

He shakes his head. "They bringin' the contract papers tomorrow."

"You got a lawyer, somebody to represent you?"

Pop shakes his head. Mom comes out of the kitchen, wiping her hands on a tea towel. She's small, like Pop, her hair still dark, a pretty face with a dimpled chin. "I tell him," she says to me, laying her hand on my arm. "I tell him, Bud, wait. Don't hurry." She turns to Pop. "But he don't listen." She smiles affectionately despite the mildly scolding tone of voice.

Pop looks shamefully at me. "Maybe they go away," he says.

"They're not going away," I tell them. "They want to buy up this half of the block and put in a mall. They're fishing, seeing what they can get cheap before anyone knows what they're doing. They get you signed up, then they've got some leverage with me and the others along here."

"Who is it, Bud?" Mom asks. "Do you know?"

"I hear Fred Pacey's one of the front men. That's all I know. You want, I can have someone talk to you, give you a better idea what you've got here. At least if you're going to sell, get what the place is worth. Make them a counter offer."

Pop looks at Mom, who nods her head. "All right, Bud," he says. "We trust you."

The Cuban toast has gone cool by the time I get back to my desk, but it is bland and my stomach doesn't rebel. Frank, of course, is going to have a fit when he learns that I want him to intercede on behalf of Mom and Pop.

And he does. "You want me to what?" he demands when I reach him at his office.

I tell him again.

"I thought you had a bad stomach. You didn't tell me your brain was affected too."

I let that slide. "Frank you're a lawyer specializing in real estate. You know what the market is in this town. All I'm asking is that you confirm that the little *groceria* next to me is worth more than Pacey is trying to pay for it."

"And what happens when Pacey gets word that I'm interfering in one of his deals, Bud? You got any idea what will happen to my career?"

"Pacey doesn't need to know. I'm not asking you to represent these people; just let them know what they've got and what it's worth."

"Bud, you kill me. Tell me how your friends are going to feel when they hold out for more money and Pacey decides he won't pay it. You think they're going to have a warm spot in their hearts for you, then, Bud?

Or maybe what you're doing is trying to queer this entire deal. Save your little shack on Duval Street, is that it?"

"Save it, Frank. And by the way, the Garcias are supposed to sign a contract tomorrow. It would be good if you talked to them before that."

"Bud, you owe me one. And don't think I'll let you forget it."

"I knew I could count on you, Frank."

He hangs up without responding.

5

◇

It is October. For many in Key West this is a time of renewal. The end of summer and the beginning of the winter tourist season; a time of green. Halloween, in fact, will usher in the first great hordes of the season, who come to dance in the streets, costumed and un-costumed, sometimes even unclothed, during Fantasy Fest.

Driving up the Keys in my ancient Buick to see Gaby, I think about Frank's advice to sell out and get away from the madness. What am I clinging to? Yes, my roots are in this city, but it is barely a shadow of the place where I grew up. I now recognize vestiges of the old Key West only in strange moments—biking by an aban-doned building that carries a memory and has yet to be renovated, or sometimes when the wind is just right and the oily scent of fish spawning is carried across the water. Moments that are too few.

The air coming in the Buick's open windows is less

humid, the sun bright overhead in a near cloudless sky.
Jets from the nearby naval air station roar overhead.

The first time I met Gabriella Wade was about fifteen
years ago. She was in her early twenties and I would
have been around forty-five. Gaby was a waitress in a
rice-and-bean joint I frequented. Right away it was
obvious that there was something different about her.
This was more than just a job. Gaby lived for her work.
She loved food. It was what she talked about. She'd put
a plate of *picadillo* in front of you and come back after a
few minutes to find out how you liked it. She did not
want to hear that it was just good; she wanted to talk
about it, analyze it. She would even suggest ways of
improving it, various sauces that might enhance the fla-
vors, sometimes bringing in something she had made at
home.

Gaby was a hit. She made eating lunch an adventure,
and it was not long before she was in the kitchen making her own brand of Cuban cuisine. Not the exotic fare
she was now serving at the Blue Moon, but she was def-
initely on her way.

Single-minded, is how I think of Gaby. She liked
men, but she was not interested in a serious relationship when she was younger. Didn't have time for it, she
said. Out of fascination I took her out for dinner occasionally until eventually it became a weekly ritual.
Dinner out. She taught me a lot about food, exulting
over watching my taste buds change as she introduced
me to more sophisticated food than I had been accus-
tomed to. Sometimes, she cooked, either at her place,
or mine.

It was after one of those dinners that we first slept
together. I was an older man who posed no threat to
Gaby's future. Good friends who occasionally slept to-

gether without a heavy emotional investment. All perfectly natural. It suited us both and became another ritual that went on for a couple of years, a passionate, but
limited affair that lasted until Gaby got her own restaurant, which took up more and more of her time and
energy. We saw each other infrequently after that, although for years Gaby would call and talk, usually about
her business, sometimes about herself, although it
seemed to me then that there was little distinction
between the two.

As I turn into her driveway that leads to a house I
have never visited, it now seems impossible that more
than a decade has gone by since we were together.

Gaby's home, like most of the houses in this area, is
on stilts, concrete columns lifting the structure above
the floodplain. It is a square, modest, frame house, surrounded by buttonwoods, silver thatch palms, and sea
grape trees, all of which I recognize as indigenous to
the Keys. No stately coconut palms or other exotics to
crowd out the simplicity of the environment.

The house is remote; no sprawling residential feel to
the area. Although other homes are around, they are
distant; the nearest is a quarter of a mile away, located
rather haphazardly. One of her neighbors, she told me
jokingly, is a doctor. In case the lunch does not agree
with me.

I can see why Gaby would view this place as a
respite, a place to withdraw to from her responsibilities
and the hectic life in Key West. It is quiet. The only
sound is that of a woodpecker drumming against a tree
limb and a few insects chittering.

Although an hour of travel time on a daily basis might
deter others, I can understand, too, how she could get
used to it, how it gives her time to clear her head, to

begin to unwind or to prepare for the day ahead, depending on the direction she is traveling.

I touch the horn to announce my arrival and notice by the car's clock that I am fifteen minutes early. Anticipation? I have to admit that my fondness for Gaby has never diminished, that I am looking forward to seeing her now just as much as I did all those years ago.

There is no sign of her as I step out of the car. The air here is different. Lightly scented and clean; no dust, no fumes, a light breeze coming off the sea. I climb the steps up to the house, where a screen door leads to a screened-in porch. I knock and look inside. No sign of Gaby. I wait and knock again. "Gaby!" No reply.

The outside porch seems to wrap around the house, which is square, not large but comfortable, its construction typical of many early Florida homes that were designed to best capture the breezes before the advent of air-conditioning. I walk around the porch to the back of the house and take in the view, which is not apparent from the front.

About five hundred feet beyond the house is the sea, the Gulf really, dotted with its many mangrove islands, like small green hillocks on the blue horizon. It is low tide, the sandy bottom exposed briefly here and there, with wading birds marching stiff and silent across the edge of the tawny flats, while above larger birds drift on the thermals along the shoreline.

Between the house and the water is a low-lying area of bedrock and scrub. It is there that I see Gaby. Or someone who I think is Gaby. She is dressed in white, some kind of a jumpsuit with long sleeves and gauntlet-style gloves. On her head is a helmet, over which is draped a veil that covers her face. She is facing a row of rectangular boxes stacked on top of one another. Bee-hives.

I lift my arm and wave. She sees me, and when she waves back, a swarm of bees lifts from around her in a golden cloud, and she begins to walk toward me, trailing bees, like a wake, until they gradually settle back into their hives as Gaby approaches the house.

6

You're early." Coming up the steps to the back deck, Gaby smiles as she pulls off the gloves, removes the helmet, and pushes her hand through her thick, dark hair.

"I'm not exactly on a tight schedule these days."

Gaby comes over and we embrace. It feels natural. She runs her hand up and down my back before stepping away. "Bud, how are you?"

"Fit as a Stradivarius."

Gaby laughs. "Doc Russell's still got the touch. Amazing. And he's almost as old as God."

"He thinks he is God."

"Well, if lunch doesn't agree with you, I'll call in Charley, my neighbor. He's young, with no bedside manner, but he's up-to-date on modern medical technology."

"He makes house calls, like Doc Russell?"

"I've never had to ask, but if it's an emergency, I suppose he would. We're kind of cut off out here, as you can see."

"I don't plan to put it to the test. By the way, when did you take up beekeeping?"

"Let's go inside. I'll start lunch and tell you about it."

Gaby takes my arm and leads me through a set of sliding glass doors inside the house. It is open, airy, and with just enough clutter of magazines, books, and papers around to give the appearance of comfort rather than disorder. A couple of deep-cushioned sofas face one another in the living room; a large bookcase is along one wall, a desk along the opposite wall.

Beyond the living room, we pass through the dining area and past a round oak table, on the way to the kitchen. Here, it is easy to see, is Gaby's life. The kitchen is bright, with windows facing south and east, lots of cupboards and countertops, and a butcher-block island with two barstools on one side of it.

"Sit down there while I go to work." Gaby pats one of the stools, and I sit down while she begins unloading things from the refrigerator. "I got into bees a couple of years ago," she says. "I'm surprised you didn't know that. I've been bottling and selling my own honey."

"You never do anything halfway, do you, Gaby?"

"What's the point? Life's too short to live it in half measures."

"But why bees?"

"Do you know anything about them?"

I shake my head, watching as Gaby dumps several containers of various vegetables, prechopped, onto the butcher block, then puts some olive oil and spices into a large frying pan on the stove and adds some of the vegetables once the oil is hot.

"The honeybee is really an amazing creature. A hive

is a very orderly and organized place. Probably because all the work is done by females. They gather the nectar, build the combs, make honey, raise the young, defend the hive, and take care of the queen."

"Sounds exhausting. And, I suppose, the male is just lying around."

"Useful only in the spring, when they are pretty much just sex slaves to the queen."

"Not a bad life."

"Except once the queen entices them from the nest, the ones who mate with her die instantly."

"Is there a message here? Stay away from a lot of hard work and sex and you'll live longer? That doesn't sound like your philosophy, Gaby."

She laughs. "Hardly. I guess I'm just impressed by their production. The queen lays up to two thousand eggs a day before she dies. And the female workers have to make about twenty-five thousand trips between hive and flower to produce a pound of honey."

"Impressive. It puts that trip to and from the Blue Moon every day into perspective."

"Don't think I don't think about that." Gaby takes a whole yellowtail snapper from a bag of ice in one of the double sinks, puts it on the butcher block, and starts to fillet it.

"Is it a lot of work for you?"

"Not really. I've only got twenty-five hives. I make sure they are in good repair and check for disease. That's what I was doing when you arrived. I enjoy it. I like watching them. In some ways it's relaxing, and like I said, it certainly puts other things in my life into perspective."

"You don't get stung?"

"Sometimes. Not a lot anymore."

There is a note of pride in her voice.

"So what's this about you getting married?"

"I want a family, Bud."

"That's news to me. Have anything to do with those bees?"

"Now, don't make fun of me. You know how I am. I put that part of my life on hold while I was getting the restaurant going. It was the only way I could have done it. I've succeeded, and now I want to move on."

"That's pretty much the way I had it figured. Who's the lucky guy?"

"His name's Roy Emerson."

The name is unfamiliar to me. "Local?"

"His father was in the navy and the family lived in Key West a couple of years when Roy was a kid. They moved around a lot, but Roy always wanted to come back here, even though he had only a distant memory of the place."

"When did you meet?"

"Almost a year ago."

"What does he do?"

"He puts deals together."

"He what?"

"I know it sounds crazy. I guess he's sort of a broker. He brings people together, you know, buyers and sellers."

"It sounds kind of vague."

"Roy's like that. He's been all over the world. He's worked at a lot of different trades, he has money, but what he likes doing best, is the deal. The art of the deal. Making the deal work, that's the way he describes it."

"All right."

"He's sweet."

"How old?"

"You sound like my father, Bud. He's thirty-five. A couple years younger than I am."

"No family?"

Gaby looks up from the fillet of fish. "He was married once. His wife died. No kids."

"Sorry. I guess I have more than a casual interest in your happiness."

"I know. That's all right." Gaby smiles. "Now, why don't you set the table. I'll just be a minute cooking these, and then we'll eat."

◇

The meal is simple. Delicious. As I eat, Gaby describes it for me bite by bite. Sautéed yellowtail in a tamarind tartar sauce, accented by red, yellow, and green peppers lightly cooked in ginger and garlic, with a side dish of plantain puree that she has brought from the Blue Moon. Nothing that I cannot eat.

Gaby pours herself a glass of white wine, California fumé blanc, lifting her glass to mine of water. "To your future," I say.

Gaby smiles, drinks. "How long has it been since you quit drinking?"

"About three years."

"Do you miss it?"

"Every day. I would love to share that bottle with you."

"Would you rather I not drink in front of you?"

"No. Facing down temptation is part of the price I pay for the years I was out of control."

"It's difficult for me to think of you like that. I didn't see it when we were spending time together."

"You're a perfectionist, Gaby. And hardest on yourself. I've never known you to be judgmental."

"The staff at the restaurant might disagree with that."

"I doubt it. I've watched you over the years. I think I know something about you."

Gaby puts her fork down, taking another sip of wine. "There's something you don't know."

"What's that?"

"You've probably never heard of Tay-Sachs disease, have you?" I shake my head.

"I'm a carrier."

I am stunned by this information, yet, never having heard of the disease, unable to grasp the severity of Gaby's revelation. "You never told me."

"There was no reason to tell you, or anyone. I'm not in any danger and neither is anyone I'm intimate with, but it's there, lurking like a deadly poison."

I say nothing. Gaby clearly has brought me out here to reveal this for a reason. I think I can guess what it is.

"It's partly why I've lived the way I have. Deferring a family life." She stares at me over the rim of her wineglass. "Tay-Sachs is rare. Infants who are born with it don't live beyond five or six. My brother died when he was five. My parents didn't know that they were carriers."

Gaby has talked little about her family. They were from Europe, I remember, and migrated to this country when Gaby was young. When she was in her teens, her mother died. I know very little about her father.

"You're afraid of having children?" I ask.

30

"I'm a carrier of Tay-Sachs. If I marry someone who is also a carrier, there's a one in four chance our children will have the disease. There's no cure."

"Have you told Roy?"

Gaby glances away quickly. "Jews are the people most at risk from Tay-Sachs."

"I never knew you were Jewish."

Gaby smiles. "See. You don't know me as well as you thought you did. I'm not religious. Quite the contrary."

"And Roy?"

"He's not a Jew."

"So you've got nothing to worry about."

"He was born in Louisiana. A Cajun. It's a weird coincidence, macabre even, that the one person I'd fall in love with and want to start a family with would be someone from the only other high-risk group for Tay-Sachs."

"You haven't told him, have you?"

"I've told him. Like you, he'd never heard of the disease. He scoffed at the idea that he could be a carrier."

"Can he be tested?"

"Yes, a simple blood test is available. He refuses."

"Why?"

Gaby sips her wine, looking thoughtful. Or thoughtfully lost. "Who knows? Why do many men refuse to be tested for HIV? Because they're afraid to confront their own mortality, or because they believe that it could never happen to them?"

We sit silently for a moment, the meal over. Gaby pours a half glass of wine.

"What are you going to do?"

She shakes her head. "What can I do? I was ten years old when my brother died. I watched him. It was horrible. The symptoms showed up when he was only six months old. He went blind, and was paralyzed before he was three. His brain was literally being destroyed, the nerve cells eaten away."

Gaby pauses, shaking her head, her expression reflecting the painful memory all these years later. "I would never have a child if there was even a remote possibility he could suffer that way."

"Roy wants children?"

"He says he does. But I'm not sure. He's different. Like me he's independent and self-made. He started with nothing. Maybe that was part of my attraction. Seeing myself in him. I suppose that sounds narcissistic."

I reach across the table and take her hand. "Call it what you will. There should be more like you."

Gaby blushes. "You're too flattering, Bud. But if you were me, what would you do?"

"I don't know. But I'd be concerned that the person I was marrying wasn't more understanding."

Gaby nods. We don't speak for a while. Finally, she says, "Well, let's move on to a happier subject." She stands up and begins to clear the table. Together we scrape the plates, clean the counters, and load the dishwasher. Comfortably domestic. Gaby talks about life out here, the remoteness and isolation that she enjoys. I watch as her spirit lifts, wondering to myself if this marriage is such a good idea.

"Coffee? An espresso?" Gaby hesitates. "Oh, sorry, Bud. I forgot. What about decaf?"

"Not for me. You go ahead."

I watch as she grinds the coffee beans. When she has finished, I tell her about Mom and Pop. We are in the middle of discussing whether I should sell out when there is the sound of a car approaching on the gravel drive outside.

Gaby looks out the window. "It's Roy," she says. "I wasn't expecting him."

8

◇

Gaby and I stand side by side at the kitchen window, watching as Roy Emerson gets out of a black Mazda. He is tall and thin with a ruggedly handsome face, the kind of face one sees in cigarette commercials. Advertising the open spaces. A man's man. He is wearing jeans, a long-sleeved shirt, and dark glasses. He stands beside the car, a thumb hooked in the corner of one of his pants pockets, looking first at my car and then up at the house. He seems to stare into the window behind which we stand. Gaby touches my arm, moving away to the enclosed porch and the front of the house. "Roy," she says.

"Hey, honey." Roy's voice is deep, rich, relaxed, as if it were filtered through an old wooden whiskey keg. "You in there? I thought maybe you had company. I was in the neighborhood. Thought I'd just drop by." He has already started up the steps.

"An old friend," Gaby says. "Come in and meet him."

Roy gets to the top of the stairs, where Gaby stands holding the screen door open. He leans forward, kissing the top of her head, one hand nestling for a moment in the tangle of hair at the back of her neck. Several inches taller than Gaby, Roy stoops even further and seems to whisper something in her ear.

Gaby turns away, blushing, to face me where I have been standing in the threshold between the kitchen and the porch. "Roy, this is Bud."

Stepping forward, I am sure that Roy has already seen me, although with his eyes hidden behind dark glasses it is difficult to tell.

"Bud?" He reaches out a bony hand. "I don't think I've heard Gabe mention you." The smile on his face is fixed, slightly crooked. He hangs on to my hand longer than I am comfortable with, gripping it tightly.

"Bud and I've known each other for years. We just don't see each other often. I invited him up for lunch." Gaby seems a little nervous, something I am unaccustomed to in her.

"You don't say." Roy finally lets go of my hand and steps back, still smiling, staring at me. "Whaddya do, Bud?"

"I'm a private detective."

"A shamus." Roy laughs and turns to Gaby. "Well, hon, I hope I'm not interrupting. This wasn't a business lunch, was it?"

"Oh, don't be silly, Roy." Gaby punches Roy in the arm, but I can see that she feels awkward, perhaps because we had been talking about him just when he drove up. "Bud was born and raised in Key West. He gave me some help when I went into business for myself. Also he plays the piano at one of the clubs in town."

"A genuine Conch," Roy says, rhyming *genuine* with *wine*. "Well, a friend of Gabe's is a friend of mine."

"He's recovering from an illness after eating in the restaurant a couple of nights ago. He was brave enough to take another chance on my cooking. I was just having coffee. You want some? Or a beer?"

Roy cocks his head to one side. "A hit of coffee. Sure."

"I should probably get back into town," I say.

"Don't rush off, Bud. I'm going to make some fresh coffee. You and Roy go out on the back deck, and I'll be right out."

"Do me the honor," Roy chimes in. "I've never met a private eye before. Tell me about it."

Before I can protest, Roy is heading across the room to the back deck, where I saw Gaby tending her beehives when I first arrived. Once outside we stand leaning into the deck rail, looking over the bay, Roy's fingers nervously drumming the rail.

"Nothing serious," Roy says, not looking at me.

"What?"

"The illness."

"Oh, no. A minor problem."

"Hospital?"

"No."

"Good. Avoid hospitals, I say. You want to get sick, go to a hospital."

There is nothing for me to say. Roy seems to have a personal issue here.

He continues to look at the water and the crooked smile never leaves his face. "The healthiest people in this country live the farthest from hospitals and doctors," he says. "Believe me. I've never been to a doctor. Look at Gabe. Never sick a day in her life."

I do not see any reason to point out that a doctor is her nearest neighbor. Or that she is the carrier of a deadly disease.

"You ever been out West, Bud?"

"Never."

"Big country out there. People live miles from any kind of medical facility. And they live a long time."

"Something in their diet maybe." I let a touch of sarcasm creep into my voice. But Roy seems to ignore it.

"Diet! That's not a word in anybody's vocabulary out West. They eat whatever they damn well want to eat. And plenty of it."

I let my own restricted diet pass. "You sound like you've spent a lot of time out there."

"Enough," Roy says, finally turning to face me. "But let's not talk about me. I want to hear what it is a private detective does."

"Right now he doesn't do a lot," I say.

"Pry a lot into other people's business, I guess."

"Mostly we just kick doors in. Shoot now and ask questions later. The way I imagine they do it out West."

Roy erases the smile for a moment. Then he laughs. "Now, Bud, don't get sore. Gabe would never forgive me. I didn't mean to needle you."

"Nobody's sore."

"Good." The smile came back. "You'll get used to me."

Somehow I doubt that possibility.

"Seriously, though," Roy continues, "you ever been shot at?"

"Yeah, I've been shot at."

"What happened?"

"He missed."

"But you've had that moment, looking down the barrel of a gun, thinking it might be your last."

Roy and I stand facing each other now. I am aware of my own portliness next to his slender, muscular frame. Staring up into his dark glasses, I wonder what it is Gaby sees in this guy. Roy suddenly offers his hand, and before I know why, we are shaking hands again. "I like you, Bud. You've got mettle. I like that in a man."

Without knowing what it was, I feel like I have passed some kind of test. Gaby comes out to the deck carrying a tray with two coffee cups, a bowl of sugar, and a small vase of flowers, which she sets on a table.

Roy goes over, kisses her again, and says, "I like your friend here."

Gaby looks toward me. I give her a smile. We both watch as Roy picks up his coffee, dumps two spoons of sugar, and stirs, then leans over and smells the flowers. "Nice. No coffee for you, Bud?"

"Don't drink it," I say, making sure I don't mention the dread diet.

Gaby stands next to Roy, sipping her coffee. When Roy has finished, he walks over to the deck rail and seems to be looking at something on the water. I watch a bee fly lazily around the porch, spinning a couple of loops around Roy's head. Roy lashes out with one hand and the bee disappears. Seconds later, Roy slaps at his neck. "Shit," he says. "The sonofabitch stung me."

Gaby puts down her coffee and goes to Roy. "You okay?"

Roy rubs at the sting. "Sure." He smiles.

"I'll get some ice and put on it."

"I'm fine," he says.

Gaby goes inside and comes back with ice wrapped in a towel. She holds it to the red welt appearing on Roy's neck. Roy smiles. "That sonofabitch packed a wallop. Was that one of yours, hon?"

Gaby nods, studying Roy, whose face has gone pale. "You sure you're okay?"

"A little weak. Maybe I'll just lie down a minute."

"I'm going to call a doctor."

"I'm fine. Just give me a minute." Roy starts to walk inside, taking a half dozen steps before he collapses on the deck.

9

◇

 tay with him, Bud," Gaby says. "I'm going to call
Charley. I think it's his day off. God, I hope he's home."

I kneel down on the deck beside Roy. Some drool
oozes out of his mouth. I reach for his wrist and feel for
a pulse. His skin is clammy, the pulse weak, a distinct
odor coming from his body. I can hear Gaby on the
phone. A moment later she is back on the deck.

"Charley's on his way."

"What's wrong with him?"

Gaby holds one of Roy's hands. "He must be allergic
to bee stings. He's gone into anaphylactic shock."

Gaby shakes her head. "Charley's bringing some epinephrine." She kneels down beside me and takes Roy's
hand. I wonder how Roy's going to feel about a doctor's
presence. Right now he doesn't seem to be feeling much
of anything; he's out like a light.

There is the sound of car tires crunching over the
gravel out front and a skidding noise when the brakes

40

are applied. Moments later, a young, confident-looking guy carrying a medical bag charges up the back stairs. Charley has a grim look on his face. He glances my way but does not speak.

With steady hands he opens the bag, takes out a syringe and a small, dark bottle; inserting the tip of the syringe into the membrane covering the bottle's neck, he pulls back the plunger on the syringe. "Roll up his sleeve," Charley says.

Gaby fumbles with the button on Roy's cuff, tears it, and pushes up the sleeve. The exposed arm has red blotches, some kind of rash.

Charley picks up Roy's arm, cradling it under his own, and searches for a vein. When he finds it, he slips the needle in and slowly pushes in the plunger. Roy's eyes flutter open and he immediately vomits.

Gaby sprints into the house and comes back with a glass of water and a wet towel, which she uses to clean Roy's face.

"What's your name?" Charley asks him.

"Roy," Roy says. "What's yours?" His voice has lost some of its timbre.

"Who's the president?"

"Clinton. I can't see too well." He seems to be gasping for breath. His eyes are hooded, unfocused.

Charley nods and turns to Gaby. "I called an ambulance before I left the house. He should go into the hospital for observation."

"Is he going to be okay?" Gaby asks.

Charley shrugs noncommitally, putting the needle back in his bag. He takes out a package of tablets. "Antihistamines. He should take a couple."

Holding Roy's head up, Gaby puts the glass of water

to his lips after Charley slips two of the antihistamines into Roy's mouth.

"His respiratory system has been attacked by histamines," Charley explains to Gaby ten minutes later as the sound of the ambulance cuts the stillness. "He needs to be in a hospital where he can have his heart and blood pressure monitored to make sure there hasn't been any damage. Two or three hours, and if he's okay, he can be released." Charley looks at me again.

"This is Gideon Lowry," Gaby says, introducing us. Charley extends his hand, giving me a perfunctory shake and a half smile, breaking away when the two uniformed paramedics come up the back stairs with a stretcher. Charley walks over to talk to them.

"What's happening?" Roy asks Gaby.

"You're going to the hospital for observation."

Roy seems groggy, weak. "Hospital?"

Gaby rests her hand on his arm. The medics come over, put the stretcher down, and begin to lift Roy onto it. He does not resist. "If you want, I can take you in with me," I say to Gaby.

She shakes her head. "I'll go in the ambulance with Roy." She watches as they carry him down the steps. "This has all been too much. What do you think it means?"

"I don't know, but I'd say Roy was pretty lucky that Charley was next door. I'm not sure he would have made it if he'd had to wait for an ambulance."

"Lucky," Gaby says. She stares out across the water. Then pulls herself together. "You can stay here if you want, Bud."

"You go on. I'll close the place up for you and then come into town. Call and let me know how he is."

Gaby smiles, gives me a brief hug, then takes off after

Roy. Charley has gone with the medics. I listen as they load the stretcher into the ambulance and then skid on the gravel driving away. It is very quiet. I take the tray with the coffee on it inside, clean up the deck where Roy vomited, and pick up his dark glasses.

Not far from the glasses I notice something on the deck and walk over to it. It is a dead bee, presumably the one that stung Roy. I wonder if it is my imagination or is the little insect really smiling?

10

The next day is idle. I have a club date, the first in several months, to play that evening at nine o'clock. After an early meal I show up at the bar at eight-thirty and find Ronnie, my favorite bartender, mixing drinks.

"Gideon Lowry," she says. "Welcome back."

Ronnie leans across the bar, and we brush cheeks. She is blond, with liquid blue eyes and a tender mouth. After five years she has become a fixture here, but despite the hours and the hazards of this sort of work, Ronnie remains without guile. She is good-natured; the late hours and often inhospitable clients never seem to wear her down.

"You behaving?"

Ronnie's lips tremble slightly when she smiles. "Ain't misbehavin'." She croons one of the frequent tunes I play. "Anyway I don't have time. Have you got your costume ready for Fantasy Fest?"

"I'm wearing it." In fact, I have on the same costume,

khakis and a white shirt, that I have worn most of my life.

Ronnie laughs. "You still on the wagon?"

I nod, and she fills a tall glass with club soda, squeezing in the juice from a cut lime before putting the glass on the bar in front of me. A dozen or so people are drinking at the bar or scattered around the room, which, with its overstuffed chairs, is meant to give the feel of a large, comfortable living room. Ronnie goes off to mix a drink. At nine o'clock she switches off the CD as I mount the stage, where the black baby grand lurks like a baited trap.

Gershwin and Cole Porter are my repertoire. I lead off with "Love Is Here to Stay," and by ten o'clock a small camp following has ascended the seven stories to the club to listen, most of them middle-aged or older, but every now and then a younger face appears.

At eleven I take a break, go to the men's room, and find Gaby at the bar when I return.

"I just got away from the Moon," she says. "I thought I'd stop by and see you before heading home." Gaby looks tired.

"How's Roy?"

"That's really why I came. Charley was right. They held him for a couple of hours for observation. We took a cab back to my place and he spent the night."

"I hope he appreciated the proximity of a doctor."

Ronnie comes by, and Gaby orders a glass of red wine.

"I guess he gave you an earful of his views on hospitals," Gaby says when Ronnie leaves.

"I got the idea he doesn't much like them."

"He was acting really strange yesterday. I think he felt threatened by you."

"By me!" I laugh. "At my age I'll take that as a compliment."

"He asked me a lot of questions about you."

"I hope you didn't answer them."

"I did. Honestly. I've got nothing to hide."

"What about Roy?"

"How did he take it? He was fine. I think that bee sting actually scared him a little."

"I was wondering if he had anything to hide."

Gaby ducks her head. When she lifts it, we stare into each other's eyes. "I've been wondering the same thing."

"Since when?"

"A while now, I guess, but until the other day I don't think I was ready to acknowledge it."

"Tay-Sachs?"

Gaby nods. "You see, Roy didn't even know he was allergic to bees. And why would he? Charley said that people can react differently each time they're stung. Roy may never experience that again, but he's got a prescription for a kit with a syringe and an Epipen with the same drug that he can administer himself if it does happen again. Just a precaution."

"From what you told me about Tay-Sachs, it isn't that random. You either have it or you don't. Am I right?"

"Yes, Bud, but don't you see, I don't know anything about Roy. About anybody, really. Except what they tell me."

"Of course."

"You said something the other day about me."

"What was that?"

"That I'm a perfectionist. No half measures. If I get into something, I'm in it all the way."

"I believe that."

"Then it doesn't make sense for someone like me to marry a guy I've known for less than a year, does it?"

"Gaby, I can't answer that for you."

"I mean it doesn't make sense that I wouldn't find out as much as I can about him. Not just because of Tay-Sachs, but everything."

"What are you getting at?"

"I want to hire you, Bud."

"Gaby—"

"Wait. I want you to do a background check on Roy. I know it sounds cold and cynical, but I'm thirty-seven years old. I don't want to make a mistake. You know as well as I do the kinds of people this town attracts. You said it. I'm a perfectionist, and I want to know what I'm getting into. It's that simple. Will you do that for me?"

I drain the last of my club soda. "I don't like it, Gaby, but if it's what you want, I'll do it. You know that."

"Fine." She raises her glass. We touch.

"Let's talk in the morning." Gaby stands up to leave, reaches for money from her purse.

"It's on me."

She reaches up and kisses me. "I hope you don't find anything," she says, and leaves.

I am not sure what I hope. Back at the piano I strike a chord and flow into "Blue Moon." Left standing alone.

◇

Around midmorning the next day, just as I am leaving with my toasted cheese on Cuban bread, Frank Pappagallo walks up the steps to Mom and Pop's. "Bud," he says, "you've put me in the soup."

"What are you talking about?"

Frank is staring over my shoulder. I turn. Pop stands behind the counter, half a dozen people crowded in the little store, waiting on their orders for coffee and breakfast. Pop grins at us while operating the big four-cup espresso machine.

"Come on, let's go next door. You want to get yourself a cup of coffee?"

"I don't want to be seen in this place," Frank says. He is excited, nervous. But that's Frank. I have never known him when he was without an edge. Although he is only a couple years younger than I am, Frank is a guy who was never expected to live long. I have known him since high school. He is someone who very much wanted to be a player, to soar with eagles, but instead he has spent most of his life like a bird in a cage, hyper and flighty. Frank is not a bad guy and not particularly complex, except when he is trying too hard to ingratiate himself. Which he frequently is.

"Frank, you ought to get on the diet I'm on while you've still got a chance."

We are sitting in my office, Frank in the big easy chair on the client side of my desk. I put my feet up, lean back in the swivel chair, and study him.

"What are you talking about?" Frank says. "There's nothing wrong with me."

"You worry too much. About other people. Stuff you can't do anything about. Sooner or later you're going to give yourself an ulcer."

Frank pushes his lips out, then pulls them back, baring his teeth. "The old guy next door turned down the offer."

"You don't say." Pop has already told me, thanking me, really, for getting involved. He fully expects to sell the place, but for more money.

"I don't think you understand, Bud."

"Probably not."

"Pacey is pissed."

"There's another guy who needs to worry about ulcers."

Frank shakes his head.

"Forget about Pacey, Frank. He'll get his store. Pop will sell, but he'll get what the place is worth."

"The word is the financing on this project is down to the wire."

"So Pacey thought he could swindle Pop, stick it to the little guy, save some dough, is that it?"

Frank looks sick. "Bud, Pacey called me. He knows I went to see Pop."

"So a lot of guys see Pop. They get coffee there. Stop worrying, Frank. What did you tell Pop anyway?"

"I told him his place might be worth more than what they were offering, but if he wanted to sell, he might have to wait to get that kind of money. The offer Pacey made was a reasonable one."

"Left yourself an out, huh, Frank?"

"I didn't think he would turn them down."

"Let Pacey up the ante. He can't just keep rolling over people the way he's done for years."

Frank shakes his head. "I don't think it's going to work that way." Something in Frank's expression troubles me.

"How is it going to work, Frank?"

He stares at me. I have never known why exactly, but I think Frank likes me. Maybe because before Carl died—my brother Carl, the state senator—he had the kind of power that Frank envies. Although they knew each other, Frank did not have access to Carl the way a guy like Fred Pacey had. So Frank was left to cozy up to the relatives, the bit players. Who knows? Maybe it was nothing more than longevity; we went back. Whatever it was, and whatever Frank's weaknesses, I did not think he would betray me. Needle, cajole, yes. But I was certain that I could trust him.

"It's hardball, Bud," Frank says, continuing to stare.

"Explain."

"There's nothing to explain. Pacey's going to put pressure on the coffee grinder."

"And just how is he going to do that?"

"I don't know. He has his ways. But it won't be pleasant for your friend."

"Wait a minute, Frank. Are you telling me that Pop's in danger? Threatened?"

"What I'm telling you, Bud, is that until you butted in, the guy was ready to sell. So you bear some responsibility. Other than that, I don't know anything. All right?"

"Not all right. The first sign of any strong-arm tactics by Pacey, and I'll be in his face like a five o'clock shadow. You can tell him that, too. As long as you're spreading information around."

"Ah, Bud, don't blow up at me. I'm just trying to help, save everyone some difficulty. You can talk to Pop; he'll listen to you. Tell him to come back with a fair counteroffer and Pacey will listen. But not the top price he's asking. Pop won't get top price for the place, the condition it's in."

"'The condition it's in' is Duval Street. Location. Remember? You told me the other night that was all there was. Location."

Frank worries his lip a little more, then straightens his tie. Frank always wears a tie, one of those old-fashioned, preknotted, clip-on jobs with a short-sleeved shirt and no jacket. The tie, red and green diagonal stripes, has a couple of stains on it. I would bet that it's twenty years old. "Forget it," he says. "Sometimes I don't know why I bother talking to you."

"You're my lawyer, Frank." I smile.

"You don't take advice."

"I'm stubborn."

Frank pushes up from his chair, groaning like a rusty hinge.

"Take care of yourself," I say. "You sound like a doddering old man."

"Around you that's the way I feel."

"Maybe if you weren't running interference for the likes of Fred Pacey, you could enjoy life."

Frank grunts, waves a hand in dismissal, and heads to the door.

When he has gone, I pick up the plastic cup Frank has left on the desk. The coffee, now the color of my khakis, has a thin scum floating over its surface.

12

◇

Gaby picks up the phone on the fourth ring, just as the answering machine clicks on. I listen to her recorded voice before she finds the switch, clicking the machine off. "I didn't wake you?" I say.

"No, I was outside watering the herb garden." She grows her own herbs for the Blue Moon.

During the two years that we saw each other, Gaby was always up early on those times when we spent the entire night together. She was not one to linger. There was always something to do. More than once I remember staggering up around dawn to find her experimenting in the kitchen. Breakfast on those occasions would be something special.

"You haven't changed your mind, have you?"

"About what?"

"What you came to see me at the club about last night."

Gaby laughs. "No, of course not."

"I didn't think so."

"You sound disappointed."

"Probably. It doesn't leave me in a very good position."

"What do you mean, Bud?"

"I mean, what if I find something out about Roy?"

"That's what I want you to do, Bud. I mean, if there is something, I should know about it."

"I know what you mean. You're in love with him."

"Bud, we have a wonderful relationship. A good time together, and he's very considerate of my time. Which, as you know, isn't easy."

"And if I turn up something negative?"

"Better to find out now than later."

Of course I knew that would be her response. Gaby is not one to change her mind once she has decided on a course of action. She does not see this as a betrayal, but prudence. And it is unreasonable of me, I suppose, to feel such foreboding about a job. But I do. "I'll need some information about him," I say softly. "His background."

"Whatever you need."

I ask her some questions and jot down the answers. Some of my questions she cannot answer, telling me that she will get back to me. I understand that she will have to ask Roy. When we hang up, I remain at my desk, studying my notes.

Roy Emerson was born in New Orleans on February 12, 1961. He is thirty-five years old. His father was in the navy, an aviation mechanic. He died about ten years ago. Roy's mother has remarried and is living somewhere in Florida; Gaby was not sure exactly where. Roy and his mother were never very close. There are no brothers or sisters. About his first wife, Gaby knew nothing. She thought they had lived in Jackson Hole, Wyoming, where Roy was involved in some kind of land speculation, but she was not clear on that either, at least not the exact dates and details.

Without a straight line to his past, or at least a solid point of entry, there really is little to go on. Roy has no deep ties to family that I can see, or any standing in a particular community. Most of his life he has moved around. He is without any sign of a continuous occupation, and that will make efforts to trace his path difficult at best, if not impossible.

Is it just coincidence, or has he lived this way for a reason? Just another footloose American trekking around the country in search of something, or someone. Typical wanderlust. Something I have never known. Without really knowing him, I have taken an early dislike to Roy Emerson, with or without the background details that Gaby has asked me to dig up.

I wonder whether it is my affection for her that has caused such a reaction to him. Maybe he was just as uncomfortable meeting me. He had come out that day unexpectedly and found Gaby entertaining me, a man he did not know. Gaby, I recall, had been somewhat ill at ease herself when Roy showed up.

Maybe Roy was simply jealous, feeling threatened, as Gaby told me later, and that was his way of reacting. For Gaby's sake I have to give him the benefit of the doubt, I suppose.

Until recently, I have done investigative work off and on over the years for the state attorney. After some political differences with the SA a few years back, that work ceased. I still have contacts in the office, however, and it is one of them, an older attorney there who has remained a good source of information for me, whom I now call.

"Bud, you old dog. How be you, brother?"

Will Seton has been in the SA's office for close to thirty years. He is approaching retirement age and has little to expect in the way of advancement or political favor from his position there. He is a willing coconspirator when it comes to dishing the current administration.

"Can't complain, Will. How's by you?"

"Oh, I can complain plenty. The word is, Bud, the head honcho here is on the way out. I know that should please you as much as it does me."

I too have heard rumors. After a decade in office, during which the present SA has run unopposed each election year, he is being challenged this year by a newcomer, someone from up the Keys, an unknown in Key West politics. Which in itself makes him refreshing. My own cynical outlook, however, tends to doubt his capacity against the political machinery here.

"You really think he can do it?"

"Between you, me, and the gatepost, Bud? *El jefe* doesn't have the stomach for it anymore. He's winding down, not putting up much of a struggle. My guess is, he's ready to bow out rather than answer some of the charges this upstart is bringing against him."

"I'm pleased to hear it." And it is good news. With a new SA on the throne, more work might come my way. Still, I know the perils of forecasting elections in this town. I will wait for the egg to hatch.

"What can I do for you, Bud? I assume this isn't a social call."

"I'm in a jam, Will. I've been hired to retrieve some background on an individual who doesn't seem to have much of a past. He's not from around here, and I was hoping you might have some contacts out of state."

"What's the name?"

"Roy Emerson."

"Doesn't ring a bell."

"No reason it should. He's only been around here for a year or so and in no trouble during that time. Of course, this is also on the q.t."

"Understood, Bud. Where do we have to go?"

"Jackson Hole, Wyoming, for one."

"Good God! That's in another universe, isn't it?"

"Couple of time zones, anyway. Can you find someone in the DA's office out there to do some legwork for me?"

"I can try. Can't promise anything."

"Billable to me, of course, and pass along my phone number. We can deal direct."

"Sure. Anything else, Bud?"

"Not at the moment."

"Well, then, as the fella says. You have a nice day."

◇

Ironically, the last case I worked for the state attorney took me to New Orleans. Because of the nature of that case I have come to think of the city—unfairly, I suppose—as a place of betrayal. However, in the course of the investigation of a murder of a witness I'd been sent there to bring back to Key West, I met a cop I liked.

Sometime before noon and after repeated attempts to reach him, I finally get Dave Robicheaux on the line.

"Lowry. Sure I remember you," Dave says. His voice, like that of a bullfrog in a swamp at night, comes across the line deep and distant. "How'd that business back here get resolved for you anyway?"

"Not in my favor, I'm afraid."

"Sorry to hear that. It was unpleasant all around. I got to know the dead kid's sister. She took it pretty hard."

"I'm sure."

"What can I do for you, Gideon?"

"Dave, I'm trying to get some background information on someone who was born in New Orleans. I thought you might be able to help."

"Sure. Who is it?"

"A guy by the name of Roy Faulkner Emerson."

"It's got a literary ring to it."

"I'm afraid I don't have much more than that to go on. He was a navy brat. I don't know how much time they actually lived there."

"Birth date?"

I relay the information from my conversation with Gaby, including the Wyoming connection.

"He have a record?" Robicheaux asks when I am finished.

"I don't know. Since you're in law enforcement, I was hoping you could run him through the computer for me."

"I can do that. One of your people could do it in Key West just as well, though."

"We're a smaller town than New Orleans, Dave. I'm trying to avoid publicity."

"Got you. Anything else I should know?"

"You ever hear of Tay-Sachs disease, Dave?"

"Sure. It's rare, but we happen to be in a part of the country that's got a higher incidence of it. Nasty business. Any connection?"

"I'm not sure, but I'd like some medical background on Emerson just in case."

Robicheaux laughs. "You don't want much, do you, Gideon?"

"You big-city fellas have resources unavailable down here at the end of the road."

"Sure, Gideon. Give me a day or two and I'll get back to you."

"Thanks, Dave."

"Nothing. I'm sure you'd do the same for me."

"You know it, Dave. Anytime."

After giving Robicheaux my phone number, I hang up, trying to think of any other leads I might follow. None come immediately to mind, so I decide to wait and see what comes back from Will Seton and Dave in New Orleans and head out to lunch.

October ushers in a different light, softer, less hazy than the hard glare from the summer sun that we have endured for so many months. Even though the weather is still hot, it carries with it a promise of relief. I can sense a change of moods. A kind of carelessness seems to have overtaken people. At the drugstore, where I sit at the counter, the banter is more relaxed, free from the edginess of summer.

When I return home, I see Pop standing in the doorway of the *groceria*. He has taken off the white apron that he wears constantly when he's working. He holds up a hand when he sees me. "Bud, can I talk to you?" he calls from the doorway.

"Sure, Pop, I'll come over."

"No, no. I come to you. Wait a moment."

He darts back into the store and returns a second later, practically running down the steps over to my place. I open the front door and let him in. He is obviously agitated.

"What's wrong, Pop?"

"Some guy come into the store and tell me I make a deal, I got to stick to deal. He got a contract for me to sign, the same one I tell you about the other day, Bud."

"You decided you weren't going to sell at that price, didn't you, after Frank Pappagallo talked to you?"

Pop nods his head. "The guy say I got to—"

"Wait a minute, Pop. What guy?"

"I don't know. I never see him before."

We are standing in the middle of my office. I put my hand on Pop's shoulder. "You didn't sign anything before you talked to me the other day, did you?"

"I don't think so."

"Then you don't have to worry. You're not obligated even if you made a verbal commitment."

"That's not what the guy says."

"Forget about him. He was just trying to scare you into signing that contract. Now, listen, Pop, I'm going to call my attorney and Fred Pacey for you. They can't pressure you like this. Who's running the store?"

"Orlando."

"Why don't you take some time off? Tell Orlando if this guy comes back to call me. I'll be around the rest of the afternoon. If he comes back when you're in the store, you call me. Okay?"

Pop nods. He must be seventy-five years old, and at the moment he looks every minute of it. "Don't worry. You want to sell, you sell on your terms, Pop."

He leaves. I sit down at the phone and try to reach Pacey. He is either not in, or not taking my call. I try Frank. "I'm telling you, Frank," I say when he answers, "I don't want Pop pressured. Pacey's already started. I tried to reach him, but he's not available. Tell him, Frank. Those tactics aren't going to work."

"Bud, I told you. There's nothing I can do. I'm out of this."

"You're the messenger, remember? So just deliver the message. And tell Pacey I'm taking a personal interest in this situation. Got me, Frank?"

"Sure, Bud," Frank says lamely. And sighs.

The rest of the afternoon I spend doing odd jobs

around the house. At four I take a break and go across to the *groceria*. I'm pleased to see that Pop has apparently taken my advice; he's nowhere in sight. Orlando is working the coffee machine. He is a much younger version of his father. "Any more unwanted patrons?" I ask Orlando.

"Nothing. Mom and Dad went home. Me and my sister are taking over."

I give Orlando the thumbs up, take a hit of the cold ginger ale, leave a dollar on the counter, and go back home.

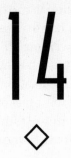

14

◇

Fred Pacey came to Key West on a millionaire's yacht
when he was twenty years old. The millionaire, an
attorney and Washington insider during the Nixon era,
was, we later learned, gay. At a time when we were on
the verge of losing the last shreds of provincialism, for
some in town the homosexual was still a matter of
curiosity and, sadly, too often animosity. Pacey was
part of the all-male crew in the millionaire's flight from
Washington when Nixon resigned. Whether Pacey was
anything more than simply a crew member, I do not
know. But, what I do know is, he did manage to borrow
enough money from his benefactor to get a start in Key
West at a time when Duval Street, three blocks beyond
the waterfront, was little more than a shuttered ghost
town.

Perhaps Pacey had a vision of Key West. If so, it
could, at least in hindsight, be described in one word:
familiarity. In Pacey's Key West there would be no

surprises. Nothing, other than the weather, that could cloud or dampen the family vacation. Key West had theme-park potential written all over it. Any threat of chaos or unruliness would be replaced by order found in the world of retail outlets, where Pacey's image of a past Key West could be marketed and sold. Slogans on T-shirts, porcelain, and plastic, caricatures and cute drawings on scraps of driftwood, would replace the real thing.

I have always preferred to give Pacey the benefit of the doubt and to think that there was no vision, that in the early days he simply began a process over which he had little control, a hit-and-miss proposition that began with borrowed money and ended in bad taste and the homogenization of a community.

Whatever the case, in 1974 Pacey purchased a couple of buildings in the 700 block of Duval, where hardly anyone except locals ventured after dark. Three businesses existed there then: a down-and-out bar, a termite-infested flophouse, and a used-car lot, which did not have a vehicle on it worth more than a hundred dollars.

Undeterred, Pacey renovated the two buildings himself, creating a modest restaurant and guesthouse that offered an alternative to the higher priced joints downtown. He went before the city fathers, begged for some decent street lighting, called up a volunteer brigade to slap some paint on the crumbling structures that remained shuttered, and slowly began the restoration process of midtown.

Ten years after he first arrived, he owned most of the block. With the acquisition of real estate also came a reputation. He was a relentless landlord who would sacrifice any tenant whose business did not immediately flourish for one that he hoped would attract more tourists. Eventually, there was nothing more than T-shirt shops competing against one another, and Duval Street had become Pacey's creation.

He married a local woman, had a child, branched out into various other business ventures, and was generally successful, although frequently despised by those who worked for him. Yet despite all that, I have never heard charges more serious than greed and bad taste brought against Fred Pacey. Which is not to say that there should not have been. Most likely Pacey has just been good at covering his tracks.

For reasons that do not make sense, it now seems that he may have lost that ability.

Over the next couple of days, Pop tells me that the pressure has been reduced to a couple of phone calls a day in which someone tries to persuade him to change his mind. Pop tells me that he has thought about it and has decided to stick to his price. If they want to pay what the place is worth, he will sell. Otherwise, he has a good business that is supporting three families; why give it away?

A kind of jauntiness has come over Pop. He seems rejuvenated by the process of negotiating, and no longer threatened.

"Congratulations, hang in there," I tell him. "You can't lose."

He smiles when Mom comes out from the kitchen and takes my hand. "Thank you, Bud," she tells me, tears misting her eyes. "A true amigo."

I hope that is the case. A certain motive for self-preservation, part of a reluctance to give up the habits and traditions of thirty-odd years, I know, contributes to my desire to see the *groceria* remain where it is. A kind of last-ditch fortification against a tide that has not only turned but engulfed almost everything else around us.

Is it pride? Am I so opposed to everything that Fred Pacey stands for that I have chosen to draw a line in the sand, to be a last holdout, and convinced my neighbor to join me in a battle that I know we are doomed to lose? I cannot say. My belief is that Pop should be paid what his place is worth and not be cheated. Beyond that, it seems pointless to consider.

Late in the evening of the second day after I have phoned him, Dave Robicheaux calls from New Orleans.

"That was quick work," I tell him.

"An easy bit of gumshoeing, and no one shot at me," he replies, his rich Cajun accent peppered with laughter.

"What have you got?"

"Roy Faulkner Emerson was born in St. Catherine's Hospital on the date you gave me. There are no records of any run-ins with the law or indications that he is a carrier of Tay-Sachs disease."

Gaby, I think, will be pleased.

"I went a step further and called the National Institute of Health," Dave continues. "They keep extensive records of this sort of thing. Nothing on Emerson."

"Good work, Dave. I appreciate it."

"Of course, you understand you can't rule him out one hundred percent. There is always a chance someone could slip through the net."

"I understand."

"The guy could just have a simple blood test and be done with it."

"I know that. He's refused. Got a thing about doctors."

"One of those. Well, good luck, Gideon."

"Thanks again, Dave. I owe you one."

"I'll collect some day. So long."

15

◇

I'm feeling a little guilty," Gaby says.

It is going on midnight. I had called her earlier and told her to call me when she had a chance, no matter how late. I can picture her now, seated at the wine bar in the entrance to the Blue Moon, staring out the window onto Duval Street, just as I am sitting behind my desk staring out at the same street a few blocks away. As we talk, I hear her taking sips of wine, trying to wind down from another hectic night.

"I wondered when that would set in," I reply, having just conveyed to her the information I received today from Dave Robicheaux in New Orleans.

"You thought it was wrong, spying on Roy this way, didn't you, Bud?"

I think about it for a moment, enjoying this time with her, late at night on the phone, something that we often did in the old days. "Let's just say I thought it could lead to complications. I'm glad it didn't."

"So I guess this means I can go on with my life, my plans." There is a change in her tone, a distance, as if she were talking from halfway round the world rather than five minutes away.

"It's a very rare disease, Gaby."

"I have it. At least the potential to pass it along to any children I might have."

"Without a blood test there is no guarantee, not a hundred percent, but the odds—" I repeat what Robicheaux told me.

"I know what the odds are. Negligible. What would you do now, Bud? Tell me."

I would wave good-bye to Roy Faulkner Emerson, I want to say. Brush him off like a mosquito. But I do not, cannot, say that. "I can't tell you—"

"Bud, please spare me." She sounds angry.

"All right. I would insist that he get a blood test. Make it a condition of marriage."

"And if he still refuses?"

"Then you have to make a choice."

Outside a car goes by, its radio tuned to an all-night jazz station. Moments later I can hear the same tune as the car passes in front of the Blue Moon.

"You're right," Gaby says. "I know. I'll tell him tomorrow."

I feel a kind of elation, as if I have won a victory even though it is meaningless, without a trophy. "Good luck."

Gaby stifles a yawn. "I'd better get up the road. Thanks for your help, Bud. What do I owe you?"

"Nothing. I just made a couple of phone calls. Someone else did the work."

"Well, at least let me buy you dinner. Why don't you come in tomorrow night? Maybe I can take an hour and we could eat together."

"That would be nice."

Once we hang up, I am restless, feeling some tension in the air. I remain for a time at my desk, then wander out into the kitchen and drink a glass of water. After playing the piano in the bedroom for a while, I stretch out on the bed and try to read. Then get up and pace.

Finally, at one o'clock, I go to bed and lie in the dark with my eyes open before drifting into a light sleep with consciousness lurking somewhere nearby. Images I cannot quite grasp seem to float just beyond my eyes. Coupled with strange sounds and sensations. I wake, then ease back into a dream.

In the club at the piano, it is crowded. And smoky. Appropriately, I am playing "Smoke Gets in Your Eyes." Gaby is there with someone I do not recognize. She is angry, either with me or the person she is with. She screams while I pound away at the keyboard, trying to overpower her, before I realize that she is not screaming at all, but singing.

I wake up. The room is dark, darker than usual. Fog seems to crawl across my vision. Not fog. Smoke. I struggle up, still gripped by the dream and sleep, and rush into the kitchen, where I throw open the back door just as a small explosion erupts in the *groceria* next door and flames leap from a hole in the roof, lighting up the night sky.

For precious seconds I am mesmerized by the lascivious flame, like lightning tongues licking against the darkness. The noise of the fire itself is surprisingly loud, and just beyond the roar, I can hear the more delicate crackling sound of old, dry timber as it feeds the hungry blaze. And then there is the smell, a combination of charcoal and burnt coffee, which, more than anything else, propels me back inside and into my office, where I dial 911, watching as the insidious smoke creeps inside.

The stream of water from my garden hose attached to a spigot at the back of the house is useless against this conflagration that grows, like some huge ancient beast, feeding on itself. All I can do is spray water on the roof and sides of my place, wetting everything down, hoping to delay the inevitable, while ash and glowing embers rain down on me like sparks from a Fourth of July celebration.

The scream of sirens barely pierces the noise of the fire. But soon there is a cascade of water pouring into the *groceria* and over the roofs of the adjacent buildings, including my own, as I stand drenched in the backyard, wearing only the boxer shorts I was sleeping in, still spraying water from the garden hose.

Firemen in heavy lime-colored helmets and jackets and black rubber boots begin swarming everywhere, some trailing hoses, others carrying axes. One of them approaches me. "Is anybody in there, Bud?"

I do not recognize him. "I don't think so. No one lives there." I realize I do not even know what time it is.

"Everybody out of your place?"

I nod, thinking about my cat, half-blind Tom, and wonder if he's okay.

As the fire begins to abate, the smoke increases, thick, dark clouds of it roiling up like thunderheads against a summer sky.

16

◇

It is five o'clock in the morning. Almost three hours have elapsed since I called 911. Although my place is untouched by the fire, when I go inside to find a pair of khakis and a shirt, everything is wet and smells of smoke and burnt wood. The electricity is off. Locating a flashlight, I make a quick search through the house to look for the cat. He is in none of his familiar places.

Outside, fire and police personnel fill the block, their vehicle lights still flashing, the great canvas hoses snaking across the street and sidewalks, while one lone fireman continues to douse the ruined *groceria,* presumably to prevent flare-ups, even though the inferno has been contained. The crowd, held back by a road-block on either end of the street, begins to diminish as the firemen start the clearing-up process.

I am standing in the street when I see Pop hurrying

up Duval. He has the look of a man who has witnessed Armaggedon. Standing beside me, he cannot take his eyes off the charred shell of the *groceria.*

I put my arm across his narrow shoulders. His face is gaunt, the white whiskers brittle in the flashing colored lights.

"What happen, Bud?" he asks in a tired, thin voice, without looking at me.

"I don't know, Pop. I was asleep. The smell of smoke woke me. When I went outside, I saw the roof explode."

Pop's jaw clenches. He lifts his hand and looks up at the dark sky. As if he could find some answer there, or accuse God. "Who did this?"

Until now it is a question that no one has bothered to ask. Was it an accident or arson? With the cleanup beginning, however, an investigation should follow. In fact, as Pop and I stand here, helpless, the question hanging between us, the fire chief walks our way, the tops of his black boots rolled down below his knees, his heavy jacket hanging open.

"Bud, what a bitch. It could have been worse, though. Five minutes later and we would have lost a couple more buildings." His face is streaked with sweat and grime. "Pop, I'm sorry. We did the best we could."

Pop does not, or perhaps cannot, speak. Over the years the chief must have had as many cups of *con leche* in Pop's place as I have. The loss of the *groceria* is the loss of a landmark.

"I understand that you called in the alarm, Bud. What happened?"

I repeat what I have just told Pop.

"You weren't aware of anything suspicious before you went to bed?"

I think back on my conversation with Gaby, then the hour or so I remained up before turning in. "Nothing," I tell him, shaking my head.

"Pop, everything okay when you closed up?"

Pop nods.

"Any electrical problems you're aware of?"

"No, I unplug everything except the coolers before I go home at night. The inspector come six months ago. Everything is good."

Someone calls the chief's name. He turns, then looks at his watch. "It'll be light in an hour. We'll start our investigation then," he says. Then walks away.

Pop and I remain fixed, watching as the firemen begin winding the big hoses back onto the trucks.

"Bud, you think this fire start because I don't sell?"

Sooner or later it has to be asked. The question of a reason for arson has been in the back of my mind, one I would rather have waited to deal with once the sun was up, the street cleaned up, and, beyond the remains of Pop's charred business, life on the block returned, as much as humanly possible, to normal. I want the chief to find evidence of a couple of crack addicts getting high behind the *groceria,* or even some faulty wiring. Anything but evidence of deliberate arson, which for both Pop and me will point in one direction. Fred Pacey. And at that time I will have to begin to live with blame, taking responsibility for interfering in Pop's decision not to sell. I am not yet ready to face that prospect.

"We don't know if it's arson yet," I tell him. "Let's see what their investigation turns up."

Pop does not say anything, but I can tell from the set of his jaw that his mind is already made up.

Dawn is breaking when I reenter my home to take stock of the damage. Which seems to be nothing that a major cleanup and paint job will not repair. But that, in itself, is a daunting task, knowing that it will be months before I am even rid of the smell of smoke. I begin to pick up soggy bits of paper and wipe a mop over the floors, leaving the doors and windows open.

At seven-thirty I give up and go to the drugstore for breakfast. People glance up when I enter, their expressions no doubt mirroring my own. Every conversation is concerned with the fire.

"Bud," one of the waitresses says. "I hear they saved your place."

"I got lucky, Mary."

She puts some coffee in front of me. I am on my second cup when Frank Pappagallo shows up, taking a seat at the counter on the stool next to mine.

"Bud, thank God you were spared."

I look at him in such a way as to let him know that the irony of his choice of words is not lost on me.

"Bud—"

"I'm not in the mood to talk about it right now, Frank."

"You got insurance, though?"

I nod, the next thing on my agenda will be to call my agent.

"Bud, you need help, a place to stay until yours is cleaned up, we've got a spare room with your own bath. Beth and I'd be honored—"

"Thanks, Frank. That won't be necessary." Until now, I have not thought that far ahead, although it does seem unlikely that I will want to stay in my place for the next few nights. The strain of sitting here now is too much, remembering Frank's warning earlier in the week. Rather than say something I may regret, I take a few more bites of food but leave without finishing my breakfast.

◇

The morning is filled with insurance agents, a team of fire investigators, and gawkers. The block is now open to a steady stream of the curious, who parade around outside, staring at the ruins. I answer the investigators' questions and sign papers while at the same time I try to reestablish some order. From time to time I look out a window and see Pop and his family trailing through the debris like scavengers.

Shortly before noon, Gaby appears. She comes in the open front door and without speaking puts her arms around me. We stand like that for several seconds, the fragrant scent of her hair and skin mixing with the smell of cold burnt wood and smoke that now seems so much a part of me.

"Bud, I am so sorry." Gaby steps back, taking hold of my hand while she looks around the office. "This is awful. What happened?"

As we walk through the house and out the back door

to look at the *groceria,* I repeat what has become a litany for me now. When she sees the charred shell of Pop's place, Gaby's hand goes to her mouth. She takes a deep breath, then asks what everyone wants to know, "Why?"

I shake my head. "No one knows yet. Or if they do, they aren't telling me."

Gaby seems to want to flee from the sight, and I follow her back inside. She is wearing shorts, a T-shirt, and sneakers. I have mopped up the kitchen, and we sit down at the table. "What are you going to do, Bud?"

I shrug. "Fix the place up and go on with my life. What can I do?"

"I mean immediately. Are you going to do the repairs yourself? Do you have insurance?"

I nod.

"Why don't you hire someone, then? Get out of here for a while until it is back to normal."

"Where would I get to, Gaby? My life's right here in these rooms."

She taps the table with her fingertips. "I thought about it on the way in this morning, after I heard the news. Bud, I've got a spare room. You're welcome to it for as long as it takes to get your own life back to normal."

"That's sweet of you. But I couldn't."

"Why not?"

"I wouldn't be comfortable with strangers working here when I wasn't around."

"You could come in during the day and be here."

It sounds tempting, certainly more appealing than staying with Frank. And I have been thinking of getting a room someplace for a few days. "I wonder how Roy would feel about that?"

"It doesn't matter. Besides I'm gone much of the time and you would be alone."

"I'll think about it, Gaby."

"Do." She stands up. "Now, what about dinner tonight? We have a date, don't we?"

"Sure."

"Good. And if you decide to stay, I'll give you the key and you can drive up afterwards."

"You're an angel, Gaby."

"Hardly. Now, I must run."

When she has gone, I sit down at the phone and call a couple of old-timers I know, guys who have basically retired from the building trades but who will do some odd jobs, part-time work occasionally. I find Gaby's suggestion that I get someone to do the renovations appealing. After the fire and a nearly sleepless night, I am tired, depressed, and not exactly drawn to tackle this project myself. It would do me good, I reason, to get away from here for a while. Bill, one of the guys I call, is available and says he could start whenever I want him. He will drop by this afternoon, he tells me, to assess what has to be done.

Before going to lunch, I gather up several changes of clothes to take to the drop-off laundry, realizing I have made my decision to take Gaby up on her offer. On my way out I see Pop standing in front of his place.

"Any word yet?" I ask him.

He shakes his head. "They won't tell me nothin', Bud. I don't know."

"I'll call the chief this afternoon." Again, I feel a stab of guilt, wanting to do something to help Pop get through this. "I've got someone coming over later to look at making repairs. You want, I can have him take a look at your place, too."

Pop shakes his head again. He seems despondent. I would like to draw him out, let him talk, but I do not know where to begin. "What about insurance?" I ask lamely.

"Some. Probably not enough."

He looks up at me then, his dark brown eyes liquid, staring. Hopefully it is only my imagination, but, I think, perhaps even accusatory. I start to walk away with my laundry.

"Bud."

I turn back. "What is it, Pop?"

"They call me again."

I do not have to ask who, merely wait. I know what is coming.

"They make an offer."

"What kind of an offer?"

"No good. Below even the first one."

Damn it! What have I done? It is time to talk to Fred Pacey.

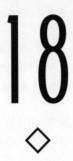

◇

The Blue Moon is crowded when I arrive for dinner at eight-thirty. There is the clatter and clink of silver and glasses above the rhythmic hum of conversation when Gaby greets me at the door with a kiss on the cheek, then leads me to a table for two in the rear. "Someone else is going to take over the hostessing for the rest of the evening," she says with a smile. "Just give me a minute and then I'll join you." She hands me a menu. "By the way I recommend one of the specials tonight. Citrus planked salmon with mango mustard glaze, cucumber-and-onion salad with black squid rice." Gaby winks and hurries away.

She knows that I am and will always be a meat-and-potatoes kind of guy. After looking over the menu with the planked salmon and dolphin coated in plantain with a tamarind tartar sauce, I decide on the grilled skirt steak, content knowing that Gaby will understand

and that I am going to get a lesson in, as well as a taste of, the other items, too.

When she returns to the table with an uncorked bottle of wine and is seated, we toast. "To your future," she says, clinking her wineglass against my glass of water. "And yours," I reply.

"What did you decide about my suggestion?"

"I'm going to take you up on it. I've got a bag with a couple of changes of clothes in the car outside." In fact, though the clothes are clean, I can still smell the residue of smoke on them, and myself.

Smiling, Gaby lifts her glass again. "I didn't think you would do it."

"I didn't think I would, either."

"I told Roy that I'd offered the invitation."

"How did he take it?"

"Remarkably well. I think he's a little shamefaced about the way he acted the other day and with what happened to him. Anyway, he's gotten very busy and won't be around much."

I nod, not at all disappointed with that news. "I also hired someone to come and do the repairs. I'll be spending most days in town, though."

"Bud, please feel free to come and go as you wish. For as long as you need it, my place is yours."

"You're very generous."

"We're old friends. You'd do the same for me."

I nod, remembering with some pleasure that at one time we were more than old friends. Gaby, perhaps aware of the drift of my thoughts, changes the subject. "What about the fire, Bud? Have you heard anything?"

"I called the chief this afternoon. He says they won't release any information until the investigation is concluded."

Gaby leans across the table. "Rumors are going around that it was set deliberately."

"Why?"

"Some developer wants to put a mall in there. They're trying to get the property cheap."

I nod. In Key West it does not take long for rumors to fly. I am not surprised to hear this, but what does surprise me is that Fred Pacey's name is not mentioned. "Anything's possible," I respond noncommittally.

"Isn't that why Frank Pappagallo brought you to dinner here the other night, Bud? To try to talk you into selling your place."

"It was mentioned."

"Bud, you could have died in that fire."

A thought that has never been long out of my mind. I have not told Gaby that it was not only the smoke but a dream of her that woke me last night. Somehow it seems like too intimate a revelation to make to her, especially in my present circumstance as her houseguest.

"What do you think I should do?"

"I don't know. Do you really want to go on living on Duval Street. It's only going to get worse."

I look at her questioningly.

"I mean the development," she says. "This street's really no longer a place to live, is it?"

"Maybe you're right."

We order dinner, and then Gaby tells me about her wedding plans. Now that Roy has agreed to the blood test, she has decided to step up their plans, which Roy has wanted to do all along. Any lingering doubts she might have had seem to have been replaced with excitement. A new venture. A new life.

When the food begins to arrive, Gaby, true to form,

tells me all about it, insisting that I taste each and every item. Halfway through the steak, however, I feel myself beginning to fade.

"Bud, you must be exhausted."

I have to admit that I could use a good night's sleep.

Gaby tells me where she has hidden a spare key to the house, and after finishing the meal, I set off up the Keys, while Gaby stays behind to close up.

The fresh air coming in through the Buick's open windows feels good; for the moment at least, the smell of smoke is absent. Twenty minutes later I am in the spare room, where Gaby has made up the bed. Unlike last night I have no trouble falling asleep.

19

◇

During the next couple of days Gaby and I seldom see one another, and when we do, it is only in passing. I spend the days in Key West overseeing the repairs, and the evenings at Gaby's, where, in peace and quiet, I can consider my options and make a decision about whether or not to put my house on the market.

Late in the afternoon of the third day, when I have lingered longer than I expected, long after the carpenter has left, the phone rings. It is Will Seton at the state attorney's.

"Bud, glad to catch you. Sorry to hear about the fire. I didn't know if you'd be living there or not."

"I'm in and out a lot. What's up?"

"That matter you asked me to look into?"

In all the confusion I have forgotten my call to Will. Or at least put it out of my mind now that Gaby seems satisfied with Roy's medical background, leaving nothing more to pursue.

"Everything's pretty much been resolved there," I say.

"Oh?"

"My client's concerns have been answered, Will. I appreciate your effort. I hope I didn't put you to too much trouble."

"Bud, you might want to call the investigator with the DA's office in Jackson Hole."

Some nerve ending tweaks just behind my eyes. "What's it about, Will?"

"I didn't get all the details, but I told him you might call. I vouched for you, and he'll be glad to fill you in. In fact, I think he wants to talk to you."

"How about giving me a clue?"

"Probably better you talk to him directly, Bud," Seton replies. "The guy's name is Don Cameron. I've got his number right here."

I write it down.

"He's expecting you to call."

"Thanks, Will. It sounds ominous."

"I don't know what you're after here, Bud. It's none of my business, but if you've got a client who is interested in Emerson, I would make that phone call."

We hang up. I sit there amidst the sawdust, stacks of lumber needed to repair siding that has sustained more than smoke damage, paint cans, and carpenter's tools. The fading smell of smoke is gradually being replaced by paint thinner. I feel unsettled. I have done what Gaby asked me to do. I should call her, I suppose, and tell her about Will Seton's suggestion before I do anything. It is her decision. But Gaby has already confessed that she feels guilty just going as far as she did in spying on Roy. If I do anything, I think, I am going to have to do it on my own.

As a friend, I owe it to Gaby to protect her. But reaching for the phone to dial the number Will has given me, I have a sense of foreboding, of stepping into uncharted waters where I risk losing everything.

Relieved when there is no answer in Jackson Hole and an answering machine comes on, I hang up without leaving a message.

Driving back up the Keys to Gaby's, I try to put it out of mind. It is possible to rationalize that everyone has something in his past that he would just as soon have forgotten. Without cause it is none of my business to go prying into Roy Emerson's life. It is Gaby's business. But because of her, I know that tomorrow I will again try to make that call.

When I turn into the drive, I am surprised to see both Gaby's car and Roy's. For an instant I think of turning around and heading back into Key West, but it is too late now, anyway, because Roy is standing on the porch, waving when I pull up.

"Bud, come on up. Have a drink. It's Gabe's day off, and we thought we'd surprise you with dinner."

Roy's rangy body presses against the porch rail while he stands grinning down at me. He looks somewhat mischievous, no dark glasses, the corners of his mouth curl upward, reminding me of a dog's expression as the animal waits for its food to be put down. Ready to devour. Gaby comes out on the porch and Roy sweeps her up against him in one arm. She laughs. "Hi, Bud."

I climb the stairs to the deck, feeling like an intruder. Roy offers his hand, and I take it, expecting a wisecrack that fortunately does not come.

"Roy got freed up unexpectedly," Gaby says. "I thought we would go out, but he insisted we cook here. You don't have plans, do you, Bud?"

"No. I'll wash up and join you."

In my room, I strip off my T-shirt, shave in the adjoining bathroom, wash under my armpits, and put on a clean shirt before going into the kitchen, where Roy and Gaby are preparing dinner.

"What about that drink now?" Roy says.

"Bud doesn't drink," Gaby intercedes.

"Oh." Roy seems disappointed. "Well, something?"

"Some club soda. I'll get it." It is one of those moments when the desire for alcohol is overpowering.

"Bud, I haven't really seen you. You doing okay out here? Anything you need?"

"Gabe told me about the fire," Roy chimes in. "What a bummer."

"The place is shaping up," I say. "Another couple of days and I should be able to get back in."

"You don't have to rush it, Bud." Gaby is tearing lettuce leaves into a salad bowl while Roy prepares some steaks for grilling.

"I'm not rushing, but I do have to get back to work."

"What are you working on?" Roy asks.

Taking a hit of club soda, I watch him. He is different from the last time I saw him. More congenial. Less combative. But I sense that he is trying, working at it. And, of course, hiding something. "Nothing of any interest," I say. "Mostly just paperwork."

Gaby glances quickly in my direction.

"I thought detective work was supposed to be exciting," Roy says.

"In books maybe."

Roy carries the plate of steaks outside to the grill.

"See?" Gaby whispers to me. "He's not such a bad guy."

Over dinner they talk about their wedding plans, and

Roy quizzes me about music. His knowledge of jazz is good, and we spend the rest of the meal talking about musicians. Something I would not have expected, and I am surprised. He suddenly seems more human, not a bad guy at all. Tomorrow I will find out for sure when I call Don Cameron in Wyoming.

20

Is wife was killed in an accident out here about five years ago," Don Cameron says from Jackson Hole, Wyoming, where I reach him the following day around noon Key West time.

"What happened?"

"No one's quite sure." Cameron's voice is without inflection, a monotonous recitation as though he were reading from a long text, anxious to get to the end. "They were hiking in the Tetons on the Idaho side in an area called the Devil's Staircase. It's a steep rocky climb, most of it right out in the open. It was late summer, and a thunderstorm came up fairly suddenly, something that happens a lot around here. Karen, that was Emerson's wife's name—she was standing out on the edge of a rocky pinnacle near the top when lightning struck about ten feet from her. Something happened. The ground shifted, a little rockslide or something, anyway she lost her footing and fell. Tumbled about a thousand feet, bouncing off rocks, to her death at the bottom."

The only time I was ever in the mountains, or saw snow, was the two-year stint I did with the marines in Korea back in the fifties. Since then I have seldom left Key West. I am a waterman, only comfortable when I am near the sea. Just listening to Cameron describe this situation sends a chill through my body. I have heard of the Tetons, seen pictures of them, snowcapped and with meadows of wildflowers, but just imagining someone actually climbing there fills me with apprehension.

"What about Roy?"

"Well, he claims he was still climbing when it happened. That he was about a hundred yards behind her. Karen was raised around here. She was an expert climber and she knew these mountains like the back of her hand."

"You don't believe him."

"Karen's family didn't believe him. They're ranchers. They own a lot of land around here and they carry some hefty influence. They insisted on an autopsy. As you can imagine her body was pretty battered from the fall. The autopsy was inconclusive, but there was the possibility that some of those bruises came before she fell."

"Meaning, you think she was pushed."

"I don't think anything. I was hired to investigate. There wasn't enough evidence to bring charges against Emerson, so the family hired me to dig into it. Understand, we're going back five years, now."

"Find anything?"

"Nothing substantive. Plenty that was circumstantial."

"You still on the family payroll?"

"It's a matter now of kind of keeping tabs on Emerson. He left here about a year after the accident. And began moving around a lot. Until eighteen months ago I was able to keep up with him, then he disappeared."

"About the time he showed up here."

"That's what I gather. I was grateful to hear from the SA down there. Is Roy in some trouble?"

"I'm not sure," I say. "His fiancée asked me to do a check on him."

"Fiancée, huh? Well, I'm glad to see he's following his usual pattern. Is she rich?"

Gaby, I assume, is well off. Rich is another category. "Comfortable, I would say."

"What with the life insurance policy and all, Roy inherited close to two hundred grand from Karen."

"Well, he was married to her."

"For six months."

"That isn't a lot of money these days."

"Precisely." Cameron lets his response hang.

Gaby's decision to speed up their wedding date was Roy's idea, I remember. "You mentioned other circumstantial evidence."

"Another accident. This one a drowning. Only he didn't marry her. They were engaged, though. Roy borrowed a bundle for a deal he told her he was working on. They were alone, a picnic near some isolated lake. She went swimming, the water was cold, she got cramped up, and before he could get to her, she was gone."

"In the Tetons?"

"No, this was in Idaho over near Sun Valley. He seems to like resort areas."

"And no inquest?"

"The woman had no close family. The inquest showed the cause of death to be drowning."

I try to imagine how I will approach this with Gaby. She knows about the wife who died, but I wonder how many of the details she knows, exactly what Roy has told her. Gaby would probably laugh at what Cameron has given me. "What's your continued interest in this?" I ask Cameron.

"I told you. Karen's family is paying me. They think he's going to strike again and that sooner or later he'll mess up. They may not be able to pin him for their daughter's death, but they damn sure want to get him. I can tell you they weren't happy that I'd lost his trail."

"I'm not sure what I can do. For personal reasons, I'm going to have a hard time taking this to my client and getting her to believe it. She's in love with him. And she's already feeling bad about spying on him to the point I already have."

"You're in a tough spot."

"What would you do?"

Cameron hesitates for the first time. I can hear what sounds like a match being struck, Cameron inhaling smoke from a cigarette. Finally, he says, "If I was in your boots, I'd make a trip out here. There's people you can talk to who can put all this in perspective rather than me just summarizing it for you on the phone. It would at least give you a feel for the situation, maybe make it easier to decide how to handle it from your end. Me, I don't think there's any doubt, Emerson's going to hit again. Just a question of time. I guess you've got to figure out your responsibility to your client before that happens."

Gaby. I picture her out there, alone in that house, remote. See her walking up from her beehives, smiling, telling me all about how bees mate, the queen leading the drones on a suicide mission. Gaby's something special. Not just a client.

"You decide to fly in here," Cameron says, "let me know. I'd be glad to meet you. Get you pointed in the right direction."

21

◇

While Bill the carpenter bangs and saws in the next room, where he is replacing the damaged paneling, I sit at my desk, stunned. It is difficult enough in this business to deal with the plight of strangers, but when someone like Gaby, someone I know and love, is threatened, the emotional toll is higher. Especially under these circumstances.

After talking to Don Cameron, I am left to pick my way through a course of action. It is clear that I can say nothing about this conversation to Gaby. At least for the moment. Not only would she laugh at me, but by confronting her right now with information like this, it would only call into question her own judgment, which would, in turn, anger her enough to drive a wedge between us. A wedge that would serve only to drive us further apart if she then confronted Roy—whatever the outcome of that confrontation might be.

In order to help Gaby I will need to continue to see

her, to get her to confide in me about the time she spends with Roy. To spy on her, in other words. And, I will probably also need to make that trip to Jackson Hole. If for no other reason than to confirm in my own mind that Roy Emerson is indeed the threat to Gaby that Don Cameron imagines him to be.

While I am trying to sort this out, Frank Pappagallo shows up.

"Bud, you busy?"

"Do I look busy?"

"A little spaced-out maybe."

"I was thinking, Frank. You ever try it?"

"I just stopped by to tell you the news, in case you haven't heard."

"I haven't."

"It's unofficial, but the word on the fire is it was arson."

"Why am I not surprised? Any word on who did it?"

Frank shakes his head. "Listen, Bud, I talked to Pacey. He absolutely denies any knowledge of it."

"You didn't expect him to admit to it, did you?"

"It isn't his m.o., Bud. Pacey's a lot of things, but he's not into burning people out."

"I'm sure you know how he works better than I do."

"I hear you put up at Gaby's place for a while."

I nod.

"You met the guy she's marrying?"

I try to keep the interest out of my gaze as I stare at Frank. "Yeah, why?"

"Just curious, Bud. He's working for Pacey, you know."

As a distraction I gather up some paper clips from my desk. "I didn't know that."

"Emerson, that's his name. He's going to close some

deals for Pacey, and, so I hear, he's investing some of his own money in the project."

I sweep the paper clips into the top drawer. I wonder if Gaby knows about this. "That's interesting."

"Yeah, I guess it is. Well, I don't want to hold up your thinking. Just dropped in to chat."

"Sure, Frank."

"Any of those thoughts have to do with selling?"

I shoot Frank the evil eye and watch him back toward the door. "Just asking, Bud."

"Don't push me, Frank. It won't work. You'll be the first to know when I make my decision. I don't want you to lose any sleep, or a commission."

Frank waves, and before reaching for the phone, I watch as he scoots up the street in his familiar, slightly disjointed walk.

I catch Gaby at home just as she is about to come into town.

"Everything okay, Bud?"

"I just called to thank you for dinner. And also for the use of your place. I'm going out of town for a while, so I'll be out of your hair now."

"Bud, you're not in my hair. You know that. I've hardly seen you. I told you that you're always welcome here."

I find myself thinking that may not always be the case.

"Wasn't Roy sweet last night? He isn't so bad, now, is he?"

I resist telling her just how bad he may be. "What's he up to these days?"

"He's signed on to some real estate projects that he has hopes for."

"Investing?"

"Roy seems to have a lot of irons in the fire. I can't keep up with all of them. I know he's invested in some things and turned some quick profits. He seems to have a knack for it."

"So financially he's okay?"

"I think so."

I try to laugh. To make a joke of it so that it does not appear that I am prying. "How about you? Are you getting involved in that world?"

Gaby laughs, too, more spontaneously than I do. "I confess," she says. "I've gotten the bug, too."

I cannot, of course, ask her how much she has invested and if she has simply given money to Roy to handle for her. "I hope you're doing well."

"So far, so good."

I want to tell her to be careful, to instill some sense of danger, but I know at this point it would be useless. And so I rely on platitudes, and then wish her luck.

"Bud, it's unlike you to leave Key West. How long will you be gone?"

"I'm not sure. Not long I hope. I'm working on a case, so it's hard to say."

Thankfully, Gaby does not ask where I am going and I am spared lying to her. When we hang up, I feel leaden, weighted to my chair, knowing that I am not looking forward to this, neither the flying, which I have a dread of, nor what awaits me at the other end of the country.

◇

The flight west is full of perils. Financial. Emotional. And not the least, physical.

On such short notice it has cost a small fortune for a round-trip ticket to Jackson Hole, Wyoming. Without a client, the expenses of this trip, of course, are all on me. Why am I doing it? To help an old friend, sure. But it is more than that. Not only do I want to protect Gaby, I also want her not to marry Roy Emerson. I know that now. Regardless of what I find out about him in Wyoming, whether he is a murderer or simply a cad, I am convinced that he is wrong for her, and I have taken it on myself to prove it. Why? Not for the first time it occurs to me that I might be in love with Gaby myself.

In the years since we were together, she has matured. The girl is gone and the woman who has replaced her is more absorbing, even more provocative. The little time we have spent together recently has produced an awkward response in me, sparking a desire that I am sure, whatever the consequences of this trip, will not be reciprocated. Nevertheless, I am determined to proceed.

Some thirty thousand feet beneath this hollow aluminum tube in which I have placed myself, I see the terrain below unfold like a slowly riffled deck of cards. The color, the texture and topography, all so foreign and remote. Once we have left the sea behind, I am, in a sense, at sea—baffled by the hills and gray wooded thickets that eventually distend into flatness and evenly marked plots of tilled earth, brown and barren, punctuated occasionally by ribbons of highway, a town, or a lone river coursing like thread, weaving the jumbled continent together like some haphazard suture sewn by a drunken doctor.

A baby cries. Someone in the row behind me sneezes. Behind the steady drone of the engines and my blocked ears, sound is strangely muted. A bank of video monitors suspended from the ceiling plays out a soundless movie while the flight attendants ply the aisle performing their strictly regimented acts of hospitality. Flying is no fun. People packed together randomly in a pressurized tin for the purpose of getting from A to B, some working on laptop computers, others reading newspapers or doing puzzles, asleep or chatting with strangers who will quickly be forgotten the moment we depart this unnatural environment.

We are chasing the sun, crossing time zones as the light outside grows brighter. At three o'clock we are scheduled to land in Denver, where I have a two-hour layover before catching my flight to Jackson Hole.

An early, unseasonal snowstorm has blanketed the Mile-High city, the pilot announces over the intercom from the cockpit. And indeed, as we cross into Rocky Mountain time somewhere over western Kansas, the world outside the plane turns gray and menacing. Thin gray clouds prevent my first view of the mountains we are approaching.

The fasten-seat-belt light comes on overhead at the same time that a bell sounds on the intercom system, and the pilot returns to announce that we will be experiencing some turbulence. Five minutes later the aircraft begins to buck, buffeted by downdrafts, unseen forces of nature, and all I can think of is that there is no visibility as we hurtle toward those high mountain ranges. Every creak and groan and change in the pitch of the engine seems to signal doom. Even the movements of the flight attendants, as they scurry back and forth picking up refuse and locking up tray tables, suggest trouble. As more babies begin to howl, the situation in Key West that has put me on this flight seems minimized, and I begin to think that I have been too impetuous. I would like a drink.

The video monitors suddenly go blank, flickering snow for several moments before being replaced by the image of a smiling, confident attendant who appears to explain the procedure for landing. But in the noise and chaos it is impossible to hear anything she says.

I stare out the window. We are descending. Watching the clouds as we surge through them and adjusting to the change in our flight path angle, I feel as if we are going faster, out of control, and when the whirring vibration of the landing gear comes on, I am certain we are speeding toward oblivion.

Images begin to appear through the clouds. I can see highways, signs of life, solid ground. We are flying across a valley, punctuated by mountains. The day is gray and dark, and I see snow for the first time in forty years, falling against the yellow-tinted mercury lights along the roads as we drift downward. For the first time in the past half hour I begin to feel that there is a measure of control being exerted over the aircraft.

When the tires thump against the runway, before gripping and settling into the tarmac like giant claws, I exhale as the engines reverse, realizing that I have been holding my breath for the past several seconds. We are down. Safe. And I have two hours to prepare myself for the next leg of this questionable journey.

Once inside the terminal, I stare at another video monitor with departure information, searching for the boarding gate for the flight to Jackson Hole. After finding it, I slide into line at the nearest fast-food joint and wait for ten minutes to get a soft drink.

In less than eight hours I have been transplanted to another world. The casual T-shirt, shorts, and sandals look of Key West has been replaced with coats, suits and ties, and more cowboy boots and Stetsons than I have ever seen outside the movies. There is something in the air, a kind of density that is unfamiliar even at this altitude. Gravity. Or perhaps it is just the grayness and cold that I am so unaccustomed to.

For half an hour I simply sit and stare at the foreigness of it all before finally trudging off on what seems like a two-mile hike to my gate.

23

◇

It is approximately a two-hour flight from Denver to Jackson Hole. I am relieved when, forty-five minutes after takeoff, the clouds disappear and we are flying in blue skies once again. So despite the agony of the previous flight, I feel a certain level of confidence return once I can see what is below us. And that in turn induces sleep, which is broken only by the announcement from the cockpit that we are beginning our descent into Jackson Hole.

As I open my eyes and look out the window, I am stunned. We are flying parallel to and at eye level with the craggy peaks of the Grand Tetons. Compared to the arrival in Denver, this is clear, clean, and majestic. The mountains are so close that I can see individual patches of snow just below the chiseled rock faces sloping away from the peaks. It somehow seems too perfect, postcard perfect.

Once we are down and inside the airport, I see that

perfection imitated everywhere. Not only on the post-cards that are in racks all over the place, but in the clothing designs and ceramic pottery that fill the gift stores. I am back in familiar territory, the world of tour-ism, albeit with a western motif.

Standing near the baggage carousel for our flight is a guy holding a cardboard sign with my name on it. He is about six feet tall in cowboy boots and a well-worn Stetson. Except for the droop of his handlebar mus-tache, his face is expressionless.

"Don," I say. "Gideon Lowry." We shake hands.

"Yeah, I kind of picked you out of the crowd as being from Florida," Don replies. There is something mechan-ical about Cameron. Maybe because nothing registers in his face when he speaks, and his mouth, hidden behind the mustache, barely moves.

"The tan?" I suggest.

"That, and you look like a detective."

"I didn't know we had a look." I certainly would never have thought of him as a detective.

"Yeah, something in the way you were taking in everything. I could tell. You don't miss much. What have you got in the way of luggage?"

The carousel is revolving now, and I spot my canvas satchel, grabbing it as it comes around. "This is it."

"Travel light," Cameron remarks. "I like that in a man."

I follow him outside to the parking lot where his Jeep Wrangler is parked and toss my bag in the back. The air is crisp, dry, the temperature somewhere in the sixties, I would guess, which for Key West would be quite cold. Here, I am sure, it is nothing. Indian Summer, Cameron tells me as I climb into the passenger seat.

"Must be quite a change for you," Don says once we are on the highway heading into town.

"I grew up in Key West, and I don't travel much. This is all new to me."

"I thought so," Don remarks elliptically. "Same for me. I've been around here all my life. Wouldn't know anything else."

I would guess Cameron to be in his fifties, but it is hard to tell. His face is round, seamless, so much of it hidden beneath the hat and the mustache.

"I've got you booked in a hotel in town. Nothing fancy. You want to change, you're welcome. Figured you'd probably be tired and want to rest tonight. Tomorrow I've got you pretty much booked up."

"That's fine."

Cameron drops me on a side street in front of the hotel in downtown Jackson Hole, telling me he will meet me here at eight o'clock in the morning, then drives off with a laconic half wave.

I stand there for a moment, feeling as if I have been plunked down in a westernized version of Duval Street. The sidewalks are wooden planks, but the shops are the same mix of T-shirts and upscale clothing outlets. Hundreds of people prowl along with cameras around their necks, eating ice cream cones, and gawking. In place of the trains and trolleys clogging the Key West streets, here it is stagecoaches. Tour busses stand at curbside, their rumbling motors spewing forth fumes, ready to gather up sightseers.

The hotel is a two-story frame building that seems not to have been touched by the renovation that has clearly claimed the rest of the town. The lobby is small, with a scuffed hardwood floor and a couple of well-worn Indian rugs around the desk and the sitting area, which consists of an old leather couch, a couple of rocking chairs, and a coffee table holding several magazines. On the walls are some mounted animal heads, deer and elk.

Behind the desk, an elderly woman has me fill out my reservation card, then hands me a key, giving me directions to my room on the second floor.

It is spare, one curtained window overlooking a back alley and the mountains beyond. There is an iron-frame bed, a mirrored dresser with a chair beside it, and, on the wall, a print of a lone cowboy riding off into the setting sun. I drop my bag on the chair and stare out the window.

It is almost nine o'clock by the time I get cleaned up and go out in search of a meal. I manage to find a café that seems to cater to locals, where I can have a steak without robbing a bank to pay for it.

Afterward, I wander around the town, trying to get the feel of the place, a sense of what it was that attracted Roy Emerson here in the first place, concluding that it must have been the real estate offices, which are as numerous as fleas on a dog. Another similarity to Key West.

By eleven o'clock, exhausted, I return to the hotel and collapse into bed, sleeping dreamlessly until the early morning, when I get up to take a leak and close the window. I have not been so cold since I left Korea. By dawn I get up, stand under a hot shower, and head off for breakfast at seven-thirty to the same café where I had dinner.

I find Don Cameron perched on one of the counter stools.

24

◇

Cameron looks up, his Stetson pushed back on his head, and I see that he is nearly bald. He nods briefly as if he were expecting me, then picks up his mug of coffee. "So you found us," he says, before drinking.

"Dinner was pretty good here last night, and the price was right."

"About the only local hangout left around here any longer."

"Tourists?"

"They've taken over everything. Not a business around that doesn't cater to them. I don't understand it. You think they'd come out here, they'd want to see something real. But no, they want it all dressed up, want it sanitized."

"We've got the same problem in Key West."

Don turns to face me, studying me for a moment. Except for a necklace made of animal claws, large claws, he seems to be wearing the same clothes he had on when he met me at the airport yesterday. Looking into his eyes, I can still read nothing in his expression.

A waitress comes to take my order. Don turns back to his newspaper folded on the counter beside his coffee cup. There is a vending box outside the door, and after placing my order, I go out and get a paper of my own.

For twenty minutes we sit side by side, reading our papers and eating. When we have finished, the waitress takes our plates and refills Don's coffee mug. Don turns and says, "You a drinking man, Gideon?"

"Gave it up a few years ago."

"May be coming to that myself. I feel like a pack mule kicked me upside the head this morning. Then dragged me across a sheep pasture."

"Don," the waitress interrupts, "you've just been living alone too long. Time you got married."

"Tried it once and it didn't work."

"Try it again," the waitress says.

"You proposing, Velma?"

"You're too hardheaded, Don Cameron. That mule needs to kick you a few more times and soften you up some." She smiles and hurries away with her coffeepot.

We leave some cash on the counter and step outside. Don pulls his Stetson down on his forehead, looking at his watch. "I'll pick you up in front of the hotel in about fifteen minutes. We've got about a half-hour ride to where we're going, and we're supposed to be there at nine o'clock."

"Where's that?"

"A ranch outside of town."

The light jacket I am wearing, in fact, the only jacket I own, is not warm enough. Even though the sun is shining, the temperature is in the mid fifties. On the way back to the hotel I stop in a store and pay too much for something warmer, a canvas coat with a plaid wool lining.

Back at the hotel I drop off the jacket in my room, make a pit stop, then go back down to the street.

Don is already waiting, his Jeep parked at the curb. "A little cold for you," Don says, looking at the coat as I get into the Jeep.

"Ah, well," I say, mocking my own weakness, "the blood thins in Florida."

"That's what I hear. Another month or so up here and you'll be drinking antifreeze." Cameron neither laughs nor smiles at his joke, staring straight ahead as he guides the Jeep along the narrow streets, where the business community is preparing for another day of tourism.

"You want to fill me in on where we're going, and why?"

Cameron stops at a light, turns on the left-turn signal, and we sit listening to its steady rhythmic click. "The Hargreaves hired me to keep track of Roy Emerson when their daughter died. I believe I told you I did that up until about a year and a half ago, when I lost track of him. He just seemed to disappear."

The light changes to green, and Don turns onto the highway I remember from yesterday coming in from the airport.

"Roy was married to their daughter, I think you told me."

"That's right, Karen. The only girl in the family, and the old man doted on her."

"And they were only married a short while?"

"Yep, about six months. Until she died."

"And the Hargreaves think Roy killed her."

Don mumbles something that I don't hear in the noisy cab of the Jeep.

We pass the turnoff to the airport, clipping along the straight valley road at a steady sixty-five, the whine of the Jeep's motor vibrating up through the floorboards. Cold air seeps in through the cracks in the canvas top. Five minutes after we have passed the airport, Don slows, making a right-hand turn onto a dirt road that can be seen stretching out for miles in front of us into low, tree-covered hills.

Barbed-wire fence encloses the grasslands on either side of the road as Don drives slowly over a ribbed-steel cattle crossing. Two great vertical logs at either side support a crossbeam in which the letter *H* is burned in a circle at its center. The Jeep bounces along the road, a cloud of dust trailing behind us.

Once we enter the foothills, the road becomes more rutted, twisting and turning, and for the next ten miles Don does not speak as he concentrates on his driving.

By the time we come to another of those log entrances, this one with a slatted wooden gate, I feel completely lost.

The sky is a deep blue and looks like something I could swim in. A few puffy clouds are low to the ground. Beyond the gate is a two-story log house, the logs a worn, rusty red. A long-haired dog comes loping toward the gate, barking. Don speaks to it, and the dog stops barking, but does not advance further down the lane toward us. Instead, he stands there watching us, his black, wet muzzle sniffing the air.

An old barn sits opposite the house, and as we drive in, a tall, thin guy with sloped shoulders comes out the wide double doors and follows us as Don drives up to the house.

"They're nice people," Don says, shutting off the ignition. "You're going to like them."

The way he says it, I don't think I will be given much choice in the matter.

25

◇

Robert "Bob" Hargreaves is tall, rangy, slightly stoop-shouldered, with eyes almost the same color as the Wyoming sky. He wears jeans, a white western-cut shirt, and a narrow-brimmed Stetson that is in somewhat better condition than the one worn by Don.

Standing on the side lawn facing the Tetons, we shake hands. Hargreaves smiles, but his eyes contain a hint of suspicion; his leathery face with its narrow hook-shaped nose is as expressive as Cameron's is absent of expression. I would guess Hargreaves to be close to seventy.

"Come on in the house," Bob says, "meet my wife and get a cup of coffee."

Don and I follow Hargreaves up the steps of the side porch, where there is a dinner bell atop a wrought-iron pole. The entire setting reminds me of any number of western movies I have seen.

We step inside a large kitchen with a long wooden

table capable of seating a dozen people. "Ruth," Bob calls out. He takes his hat off and puts it on an antler rack just inside the door. His hair is thick and perfectly white.

Moments later a woman enters the kitchen, says hello to Don, and offers me her hand as Bob introduces us.

Like her husband, Ruth is slender, well kept, with short, gray hair and friendly dark eyes. She wears a peach-colored shirt-style blouse tucked into a long denim skirt. Silver bracelets adorn one arm. "Go on in the front room," she tells us, "and I'll bring out some coffee. Would you like something to eat?"

"Thanks," I say, "but I just had breakfast. And I don't drink coffee."

"Anything else?"

"A glass of water would be fine."

"You got any of those good cinnamon rolls, I wouldn't say no to one," Don says.

Ruth laughs as Bob ushers us into the living room, a vast room with a beamed ceiling, wide plank floors covered with colorful Indian rugs, two leather couches facing one another in front of a wide plate-glass window framing the ever-present Tetons. At one end of the room a stone fireplace big enough for a small man to stand upright in has the still glowing embers from a recent fire. A bar complete with barstools occupies the opposite end of the room, and suspended above it all, from the centermost ceiling beam, a wagon-wheel chandelier.

"Quite a place," I remark as we sit down on the couches, Bob and Don sitting opposite me. Don crosses one leg over the other and puts his hat on his knee.

"My grandfather built it in the mid 1800s," Bob

replies proudly. "Except for four years away at school and a brief tour in the army, it's the only home I've known. We've added onto it and of course modernized over the years, but essentially it's the same place it was a hundred and fifty years ago."

Ruth brings in a tray with a silver coffee urn, four cups, and a plate with a couple of cinnamon rolls dripping with melted butter.

"Will that keep you going, Don?" Ruth asks.

"Until lunch," Don replies.

Ruth shakes her head, hands me a glass of water, then sits on the couch beside me, and begins to pour coffee. "Don is like family," she explains. "In fact his own family had the ranch next to ours for many years."

"Until it was foreclosed," Don says.

There is a brief silence before Bob speaks. "Well, we're all going down the drain," he says, "with the government cutting grazing land and the price of cattle what it is. Not to mention taxes as the land gets more valuable to the recreation community."

Ruth finishes pouring and passes out the coffee.

"What are you going to do?" I ask, thinking about my own small crisis at home, whether or not to sell out in the face of the unstoppable march of tourism.

Bob's head droops forward on his chest for a moment. Ruth stares at him. "Don't know," he says. "And don't guess it makes too much difference, since we won't be here, anyway."

"Oh, don't be so morbid, Bob." Ruth puts a roll on a saucer and hands it to Don. "What he means is," she says, turning to me, "is that we've got two sons, and neither one of them is much interested in ranching."

Bob lifts his head. "Karen would have been the rancher. She loved this place."

Ruth shakes her head. "Honey, you know a woman can't run a spread like this."

"She could have. If she'd had the right man helping her."

"That girl knew what she was doing when it came to horse sense," Don remarks.

"She ought to," Ruth says, "she was raised on one. But riding a horse isn't all that ranching is about; you know that, Don Cameron."

"Well, I don't know. Women are different these days, Ruth. They can pretty much do whatever they want to do, even if it is traditionally a man's job."

"That's right," Bob echoes. "Karen could have managed this place, and I was ready to let her."

"What do your sons do?" I ask.

Bob waves a hand in the air. "They're in town. One of them's gone into real estate, and the other's practicing law."

"They're both good boys," Ruth adds somewhat defensively. "It can be a real hardship out here at times. Cut off from people, from any kind of a social life." She sounds wistful.

"If you want to call what Jackson Hole's turned into a social life," Bob says.

"Oh, honey, you know what I mean."

Bob nods, smiling at his wife. "You don't have any complaints at this late date, do you?"

Ruth smiles back. "None. But in that regard I think I can perhaps understand the boys better than you can."

Don has finished his cinnamon roll and wipes his mustache on one of the paper napkins Ruth gave him. "Gideon here knows Roy Emerson," he says. "He's down in Key West about to get married again."

Hargreaves stands up and walks over to the picture window, standing with his back to us, part of the scenic mountain setting now. "I'll see that man in hell," he says so softly I can barely hear him.

Ruth puts a hand to her eyes, shaking her head.

26

◇

Getting up from the couch, Ruth walks to the fireplace and returns with a framed photograph. "This is Karen," she says, handing me the color photo of a pretty young woman standing in a high meadow with snow-capped mountain peaks behind her. She is wearing shorts and hiking boots, the straps of a backpack clearly visible around the shoulders of her sweatshirt. She carries a walking stick. Despite the snow on the mountains, the meadow where she stands is filled with wildflowers in bloom.

"She knew the Tetons like the back of her hand," Bob Hargreaves says, turning from the window. "She had hiked and climbed in these mountains ever since she was old enough to walk."

Like her mother, Karen has an oval face. Her hair is blond, cut shoulder length and pulled back from her face with a red band. She is smiling. There is nothing in her expression to suggest anything other than youthful excitement and confidence. She appears happy and in good health.

"That was one of the last pictures of her ever taken." Ruth pours more coffee into Don's cup.

"Who took the picture?" I ask.

"Roy." Ruth barely whispers the word, as if it is forbidden.

"Were they married then?"

Ruth nods. A quietness has come over the room. I try to imagine Bob and Ruth's life here now in this big house, remote, alone.

"How did they meet?"

Bob moves away from the window and walks toward the kitchen.

"Karen's brother introduced them. Jim." Ruth continues to speak in a hushed tone of voice.

"Which brother is that?"

"The one in real estate."

Don picks up his coffee cup and carries it into the kitchen. As Ruth tells me how Roy and Karen first got together, I can hear the indistinct voices of Don and Bob conversing in the other room. Roy, Ruth tells me, was in some development deal that her brother Jim had an interest in. Ruth has forgotten the exact details, it was more than five years ago, and anyway she thinks the deal fell through.

"How long after they met before they got married?"

Ruth looks down, smoothing her skirt. "About a year, I think."

"And how long were they married?"

"Six months."

I think of Gaby. She, too, has known Roy only about a year. "What happened?"

Don has already given me the details of Karen's death,

but I listen again as Ruth repeats essentially the same information. A hiking trip on the Idaho side of the Tetons in late summer. A sudden thunderstorm with Karen standing on a rocky pinnacle when lightning struck not far from her. Something happened. She lost her footing. And fell. Nearly a thousand feet straight down. Ruth does not look at me. Her voice breaks.

Staring at the picture of Karen I hold in my hands, I find it difficult to imagine her terror. She seems so composed, so sure of herself. In that way, at least, like Gaby.

"And Roy wasn't around," I say.

Ruth shakes her head. "So he said."

I continue to study the photo while Ruth appears to withdraw inside herself. Bob and Don reappear from the kitchen. Bob walks with a distinct gait, as if his knees are bad. "I can tell you this," he says, going to stand by the fireplace, where he examines the many photos that are lined up there. I assume most of them must be of Karen. "She would never have been standing out there in the open, exposed, when a storm was blowing across. A year doesn't go by around here that somebody isn't struck by lightning. Usually a tourist, someone inexperienced in the mountains. That wasn't Karen."

"What would she have done?" I ask. "Caught out like that."

"Found a rock, a ledge, a cave. Someplace to crawl in or under. She would not have just been standing there."

I nod. "What do you think happened?"

Leaning against the mantel, Bob Hargreaves shakes his head. "I know what happened. The sonofabitch pushed her."

"Bob," Ruth says.

It is unclear if she is admonishing him for his language or the accusation, but her husband does not respond.

"What would his motive have been?" I ask. "Why did he push her?"

Bob and Ruth look at one another. Don moves back around to the couch facing me. "Roy took out a life insurance policy on Karen against accidental death," Don says. "A hundred grand."

"He had also borrowed that much, or more, from her after they were married," Bob adds.

"Karen had that kind of money?"

"All the kids had a trust fund. When she turned twenty-one, Karen had access to a quarter of a million dollars."

"What did Roy want the money for?"

"Investments."

"Did Karen talk to you about it?"

"We have always tried not to interfere in our children's lives," Ruth says. "Karen didn't consult us about it. We found out only after her death."

"Did you get the money back?"

"No," Bob says sharply. His blue eyes have turned to ice. "And we won't get Karen back, either."

"You requested an inquest?"

Don clears his throat. "It was inconclusive, Gideon." He stares at me as though he has more to say but is reluctant to say it, and it is clear that he wishes I hadn't brought the subject up again. I assume out of deference to the Hargreaves.

"Then no charges were brought against Roy, I take it?"

They all shake their heads. "He left town about three months afterwards," Don says. "Once the paperwork was done and he had collected on the insurance."

We sit in silence again. My mind turns back to Gaby, and I picture Roy standing on her deck, railing against doctors and hospitals, while extolling the folks in this part of the country for their independence from medical institutions. I also begin to picture him alone with Gaby, remote and isolated. I wonder what I am doing here.

"You're probably wondering what can be done, why I thought it would be a good idea for you to come out here," Don says.

"It did cross my mind."

"We think he's going to strike again, that Karen's death wasn't an isolated event but part of Emerson's m.o."

Hargreaves limps back over to the window. "We may not be able to get him for Karen's murder, but . . . well, we understand from Don that you were checking up on him."

"Roy is planning to get married again. His fiancée wanted some medical history on him. I provided that. This other came right out of the blue."

Bob smiles understandingly. "After Karen's death we hired Don to investigate. You probably know that."

I nod.

"But he's got a job with the DA's office. There was only so much he could do."

"At this point there's only so much anyone can do," I reply.

"But you're living in the same town now. You know the woman he wants to marry."

Again, I nod.

"We wanted to meet you, talk to you. Which is why I asked Don to try to get you out here. You must have had some concern because you were willing to come all the way up here on your own."

I don't say anything. There is a long silence.

"Well, we want to make it worth your while. I'd like to pay for your expenses and hire you to do what Don here was doing, keep track of Emerson as long as he's in your part of the country. Maybe we can save someone else."

"Save someone?" I ask. "Or, bring him down for what happened to Karen?"

Hargreaves turns away, staring out the window. Don sits stroking his mustache. Ruth carries the tray back into the kitchen. "Maybe it looks that way to you," Bob says. "It's true, we want to see justice served."

"Without clear evidence against him?"

Don clears his throat again.

"We're not asking you to do anything illegal."

"I had to make sure," I reply.

"Believe me, we don't want to see anyone else go through what we have."

"I don't either," I say.

27

◇

In low gear Don Cameron's Jeep grumbles and growls along the rutted road back toward town. Don does not speak until we reach the blacktop a couple of miles from the Hargreaves's home. A check for a thousand dollars, folded once, reposes nicely in my shirt pocket.

"Didn't I tell you they were good people?" Don shifts into fourth gear as the wide-tread tires begin to whine against the smooth blacktop.

I agree they seem like good people. There is something about Bob Hargreaves, some quality in him, that resonates with me. "At their age, isn't it tough living all alone up there?"

"You get used to it." Something in Don's voice sounds a little wistful. "The winters are the worst. Hell, forty years ago you could get snowed in for three months. In bad winters there were a lot of times I had to ride a horse to school. Now the roads are pretty much kept clear and you can get to town whenever you want. But

Bob and Ruth like it up there. They don't really come down any more than they have to."

"I guess that your families were close."

Don grunts. "I've known the Hargreaves all my life."

"When did you move into Jackson?"

"When I was fifteen. My old man died and left us with a lot of debt. It was just my mother and me to work the ranch, so we didn't have much choice. We sold what we could to the Hargreaves and the creditors got the rest. My mother went to work in a bank in Jackson. Summers I worked for the Hargreaves."

Some little whisper of an idea trips across my brain. "How well did you know Karen?"

Don turns his head sharply toward me for a second, and I sense that I have touched a raw nerve. "We were friends even though she was ten years younger than me."

Something in his manner prompts me to tell him about Gaby. When I finish, we ride in silence for a while. "Curious," Don finally says.

"What's curious?"

"I was crazy about Karen." Cameron looks out the side window, watching a guy in waders fly-fishing in a stream.

"I thought maybe you were."

"For a few years we spent a lot of time together. Friends, you know. We had a lot of the same interests, but when it came down to anything more than that, the age difference was just too much."

"But you had hopes."

Don shrugs. "The heart mends."

I recall the conversation with the waitress earlier this morning. "But you never found anyone else like her."

Don runs a hand over his bushy mustache. "Never."

"Did you meet Roy?"

Don shakes his head. "Didn't want to. But by the time he came on the scene, Karen and I had gone our separate ways, anyway."

"What was her attraction? To Roy, I mean."

"I've thought about that. Karen loved it here, this valley, even with all the changes. She never grew tired of it, or cynical, the way some of the rest of us have. I guess she was able to adapt better than I ever could. That isn't to say she approved of what was happening here, but she knew how to live with it, and make the most of it. Me, I would just retreat, go back to the mountains and live much the way Bob and Ruth do now. If I could. Karen, on the other hand, wanted to be in on everything. She liked newcomers, welcomed their ideas. I think that was what it was with Emerson. He came from the outside world with a different point of view and plenty of charm. Damned if I know what it was, but Karen fell for him."

Just like Gaby. "Do you think she really would have run the ranch?"

A nerve in Don's jaw twitches, pulling at one side of his mustache. He nods. "I think so. I doubt that Emerson would have lasted."

"But she couldn't have done it on her own."

"She would have had help."

"From you?"

"The offer was always there."

We ride in silence again for a while. "Tell me about the necklace," I say.

Don lifts a hand and fingers the claws around his neck. "From a bear," he says. "The last one I ever shot."

"You're a hunter?"

"Nope. The year my dad died a rogue griz got into

our cattle and killed a couple of the heifers. I tracked it down and shot it." Don speaks matter-of-factly, slowing the Jeep as we approach the intersection with the highway into town. "Today you hardly ever see a griz around here. Some over in the park, in Yellowstone, of course, but with all the development around Jackson, they're getting pushed out like everything else. A dying breed, I guess you could say."

"Like you and me, maybe."

Don turns and looks at me. "Maybe," he says. "People have gotten so used to seeing nature bottled and corked that they forget there is still stuff out there that can kill you."

It is approaching one o'clock when we reach town. Don suggests lunch, and we go back to the same café where we had breakfast.

"I take it you've got something lined up for this afternoon."

"Yep," Don says. "I want you to meet Karen's brother Jim."

"The one in real estate?"

Don nods as the same waitress who served us this morning approaches. "Let me guess," she says. "Chicken fried steak."

"Gravy on the mashed potatoes," Don answers.

She looks at me. I have never eaten chicken fried steak. "Double that order," I say.

28

◇

Snake River Realty is a chic weathered frame building sandwiched between an art gallery and a factory outlet clothing store. The windows of the gallery are filled with large, lifelike paintings of Indians in headdress and war paint, and on pedestals beside them bronze sculptures of cowboys on broncs—modest imitations of Remingtons.

The realty office is like all realty offices everywhere, functional, without unnecessary accoutrements. It is instead entirely devoted to the business of selling houses. One front window panel is given over to color pictures of properties for sale, some with "sold" in bright red letters stamped diagonally across their faces. A quick glance at the price list reveals that Jackson Hole has more than tourism in common with Key West.

Inside, a secretary is seated at an unadorned desk. When she looks up, Don tips his Stetson. "Don Cameron," he says. "We've got a one-thirty with Jim."

The secretary, a middle-aged blond woman wearing a fringed shirt and a bolo tie with a large turquoise clasp, looks at her watch, then picks up the phone, speaking into the receiver, her chin tucked down, in a voice apparently meant to be heard only by whoever is on the other end of the line. When she hangs up, she looks up, smiling brightly, with little half moons of flesh appearing on either side of her mouth. "He'll be right out," she says.

Don seems nervous, uncomfortable, as if he feels out of place here. I can't say that I blame him. Five minutes later, when I hear a door opening and closing, we both peer expectantly down the hallway leading toward the back.

"Don, how you doing? Long time no see." The man who appears, offering his hand, first to Don, then me, is tall, slender, dressed in a business suit with a white shirt and tie. Shiny tasseled loafers on his feet replace the ubiquitous boots.

"Gideon Lowry," Don says. "Jim Hargreaves."

Except for the hawklike nose and sky blue eyes, Jim appears to have little in common with his father. He projects a certain sophistication at odds with the easy-going western informality that seems so much a part of his parents and Don Cameron. Behind the suit and cool eyes, I sense some unexplored tension in Hargreaves.

"Let's go back to my office," Jim says. "Can I get you anything?"

"Nothing for me," I reply.

Don shakes his head.

"Carla, hold all my calls."

The secretary nods, while using one lacquered thumbnail to squeeze a mint from a paper roll.

Hargreaves's office is large enough to accommodate a desk and a conference table. On the table are several blueprints. Hanging on the walls, framed black-and-white photographs depict Jackson Hole in its various stages of development. Hargreaves pushes the blueprints to one end of the table and sits down at the other end, Don and I taking seats opposite one another on either side of him.

"We were up at the ranch earlier," Don says.

"Mother called and told me." With a forefinger Jim worries the cuticle of his thumb. He looks at me. "She said Dad hired you to look into Karen's death."

"I gather that's been pretty well examined," I reply. "What they hired me to do is keep an eye on Roy Emerson."

Hargreaves shakes his head disapprovingly. "You probably won't agree, Don, but I think this whole thing has gotten to be rather obsessive on their part."

Cameron lifts his Stetson and runs a hand over his smooth head, dropping the hat on the table. "I don't know about that, Jim."

"Karen's been dead five years now. There was never anything except Dad's hang-up on this issue to keep this pursuit going. Not a whit of medical evidence to suggest Karen's death was anything but accidental."

Don shrugs. "Gideon's from Key West, Florida. He got in touch with the DA's office here looking for some background information on Emerson. I asked him to come out here. I thought it might be good if he talked to your parents. Good for them at least."

Hargreaves shakes his head again, turning to me. "Roy's in Key West?"

"Been there about a year now."

"What's he doing?"

"I'm not sure. Investments. Real estate. It isn't too clear exactly what he does. But he is getting married again soon."

A slight smile creases Hargreaves's smooth face. "How can I help you?"

"You did know Roy, didn't you?"

"Sure, I knew him. I introduced him to Karen. Don must have told you that."

I nod. "I'm curious about your relationship with Roy."

"We worked on a project together. I liked him. He was smart and had a talent for bringing people together and getting things off the ground."

"What was the project?"

"A development just outside town. It was meant to be a trading post with a variety of shops and a motel attached, along with a theme park where the kids could hang out. We were even going to have wild animals in pens. A bear or two, and buffalo, that kind of thing. For those people who didn't want to traipse through Yellowstone looking for them in the wild."

Apart from the animals, the very sort of thing that Key West now trafficks in. The kind of insipid nonsense that has ruined a perfectly real town. Don sits with his hands folded over his belly, looking like a cowboy Buddha. Though he doesn't say anything, I can just imagine what he's thinking. Bears in a pen!

"Did Emerson invest in it?"

"Roy was the principal. He had the thing put together in record time. Met with officials to get the variances and paperwork needed. He did it all."

"Can I see the results?"

"Unfortunately, not. The place burned before it was half completed."

"Do tell," I say. "Roy held the insurance papers on it, I suppose."

Jim Hargreaves nods.

29

◇

Jim Hargreaves is right. There is nothing in any of this to accuse a man of murder, even arson, much less convict him of either. Still, I feel the urgent need to talk to Gaby, and this isn't going to be easy. Somehow I must convey enough of what I have learned to let her know that she should proceed cautiously with Emerson—but without having her feel that I am advising her to end that relationship or that I have taken it upon myself to interfere in her personal life. Not without more hard evidence.

It isn't going to be easy.

Jim Hargreaves regrets introducing his sister to Roy Emerson, he remarks. "Roy is a scoundrel. No doubt in my mind about that. A charming scoundrel, too. Maybe the worst kind. But I'll be damned if I am convinced that he's capable of murder."

"Arson?"

Hargreaves lifts his hands. "I don't know."

There seems to be nothing left to say. Don fiddles with the brim of his Stetson. "On what terms did you and Emerson end up?"

Jim seems to suppress a laugh. "My sister is dead, and he cost me nearly a hundred grand. How do you think we ended up?"

"Did the two of you talk before he left town?"

"No. As far as I know no one knew he was leaving. He just vanished one day."

"Didn't you think that was a little suspicious?"

"I don't think Roy Emerson had a lot of credibility left in Jackson Hole."

I nod, considering further questions. I have a check in my pocket, a case I am now being paid to investigate. Despite his feelings about Roy, Jim Hargreaves has made it clear that he would not approve this investigation. My chair squeaks against the tile when I move it to get up.

"I'm sorry I can't be of more help," Hargreaves says, standing.

I shrug, watching Don Cameron push his bulk up. The three of us shake hands, and Don and I leave. Outside, we stand on the boardwalk beneath the overhang above the porch for a moment.

"You don't like him, do you?" I ask Cameron.

"I don't have strong feelings about him one way or the other. Growing up, Jim and Karen were close. I think he tried to influence her away from the ranch."

"Why?"

"Hell, the same reason you'd influence anyone you loved away from that line of work. No future in it."

"And yet you'd go back to it in a heartbeat?"

"It's a way of life. Karen had it in her blood. The boys

133

for some reason didn't. That shit about trading posts, theme parks, and bear pens. That's where the future is."

"But you already told me you thought Karen would have run the ranch."

Don begins walking back toward the Jeep. "I've heard rumors that the boys would like to have seen the place turned into a guest ranch."

"Meaning?"

"Meaning once Bob and Ruth were gone, the ranch would be managed for paying guests. Dudes, they used to call them. People who'd never been on a horse, rich folks who would be willing to pay a fortune for a couple weeks in the mountains."

"You don't approve?"

"I don't know what it's like in your part of the country, but out here no one much cares what anyone thinks beyond the immediate concern of making a buck as fast as they can and any way they can."

"I'd say that was true in Key West."

"Take folks like Roy Emerson. The guy comes in, contributes to ruining a place, and succeed or fail, he's off to the next place."

"Sounds familiar."

"My guess is they tried to persuade Karen to run the ranch on those conditions and she said no."

"What about Bob and Ruth?"

"If all three kids were behind it, I suppose the thinking was their parents would go along with it. Given their age and the circumstances."

"What happened?"

"Karen wouldn't do it."

As I weigh the consequences of this remark, a stagecoach goes by, pulled by four roan horses, their heads down and wearing blinders, while the driver, decked out in woolly chaps and a high-crowned Stetson, beseeches passengers.

"You talked to Karen about this?" I ask Don, watching the progress of the stagecoach.

"I told you. I'm guessing. But it's something to think about."

Back at Cameron's Jeep, I start to climb in until Don stops on my side and leans up against the Jeep's front fender. "Here's the deal," he says. I close the door. "I can take you over to the medical examiner and you can talk to him, question him about Karen's death."

"You've already done that."

"That's right. I've got his reports and I can tell you what he said. But it's your case now. I want to give you the option to ask your own questions."

I shrug. I do not doubt Cameron's ability. With the years that have passed since this was first investigated, I can't imagine I would be able to dig anything fresh from the M.E.

"Fine," Don says. For the first time a trace of a smile plays in his eyes. "You don't mind joining me at the bar, I could use a beer." He looks at his watch. "A mite early, but this has been a troubling day."

The bar is across the street from where the Jeep is parked. Off the beaten track. An old weathered joint without the chic. A scarred mahogany bar, wooden barstools, and a mirrored back bar, the only accessories. The walls are filled with mounted trophy heads of deer, elk, and antelope—their tawny coats dusty and their big glassy eyes shining like gemstones.

"Don," the bartender greets him, and places a mug of draft beer on a mat in front of him before turning to me. "What can I get you?"

"Club soda."

He walks away, returning moments later with a tall glass of fizzy water. He chats with Don for a moment, then leaves to tend another customer.

"Well, you've gotten the picture," Don says after a short sip of beer.

"Such as it is."

"You see why I was anxious to get you out here. This couldn't have been done on the phone. Bob and Ruth aren't that kind of people. They needed to look you in the eye. You measured up. They like you."

"For whatever it's worth."

"If nothing more, you've got your expenses covered and been paid for some of your time."

"Now what I need is some hard evidence. Something more than conjecture."

"I know. I wish I had it to give. I don't. But there is more circumstantial stuff."

"Like what?"

Don takes another pull from the mug. Then, wiping foam from his mustache, says, "The other victim."

Even though he mentioned the drowning when we first spoke on the phone, a tingle passes across the back of my neck like a chill. "When was this?"

"Three years ago. More than a year after Karen's death."

"Where?"

"Over in Idaho. Sun Valley. Another resort town."

"Tell me again what happened."

"A woman drowned. She and Roy were engaged. They were alone, on a picnic at an isolated lake. She went swimming, the water was cold, she cramped up, and before he could get to her, she was gone. That was his story."

"You investigated?"

"I drove over there, about a day's drive from here. The woman had no close family. There was nothing in the inquest to suggest it happened other than Roy described it."

"Motive?"

Don shakes his head. "They had a joint bank account. Apparently the woman had inherited some money, substantial, but not a lot. Of course, it went to Roy."

Once again my mind races back to Gaby. Alone in her house. Remote. Telling me how bees mate, the queen leading the drones on a suicide mission. Then Roy comes into the picture.

30

◇

At nine o'clock mountain time, given the two-hour time difference between Jackson Hole and Key West, I begin calling Gaby. I do not expect her to be home from work yet, so it is no surprise when the answering machine clicks on, and I hang up. I have deliberately chosen not to call Gaby at work. Having no idea what I will say to her, if anything, about Roy. But, with a mixture of pleasant anticipation and anxiety, I look forward to one of our late-night calls.

Don is on his third beer when I leave the bar. It is after sunset, quickly growing dark, and along with the drop in temperature, the wind has come sweeping into the valley carrying the icy chill of winter. Don proposes driving across the pass into Idaho tomorrow and hiking up the Devil's Staircase. In this thin air, my breathing is labored enough without my having to undergo a rigorous mountain-climbing expedition. Besides, I can see little to be gained. We agree, however, to meet for breakfast in the morning and determine our next move then.

After leaving Don, I go to the café and eat a bowl of chili before returning to my room, where I am free from the knife-edged wind and raw, burning cold.

At nine-thirty, I try Gaby again. Still getting only the answering machine. Restless, I walk down to the lobby, where a fire burns in the fireplace and the TV is on. Plopping down in one of the easy chairs closest to the fire, I watch a mindless sitcom, along with the elderly receptionist, who smiles at the TV banter.

It is somehow comforting here, the sitcom a distraction that momentarily keeps the worry at bay. Perhaps that's what this kind of program is designed for.

Shortly after ten, when the news comes on, I go back to my room. It is now after midnight in Key West. Gaby is still not home. It is possible that she has gone out for a drink before driving back to Sugarloaf, or perhaps she has stayed in town with Roy. In any case, it is too late to call again tonight.

A book that I brought with me on the plane, but was too nervous to read, is on the beside table. Entitled *Marquesa,* it describes six weeks in the life of its author, Jeffrey Cardenas, alone on a houseboat in the backcountry, the uninhabited islands of the Marquesas west of Key West. The descriptions of warm water and sky and fish make me homesick. After a couple of hours reading, I fall asleep and dream of the sea.

When the dream turns to a nightmare, I awake and read the luminescent hands on my watch. It is six o'clock, still pitch black beyond the window, where the mountains loom. Gaby was in the dream, caught in some swift outgoing tide, the swirling currents carrying her seaward as she struggles to get back to shore, where

I watch helplessly. But the watching face turns from mine to Roy's. Grinning that crooked grin.

After peeing, I rinse my face in water so cold it feels as if it is straight from the fridge. Then go back and sit on the edge of the bed and reach for the phone. It is after eight in Florida. I dial Gaby's number, once again getting the answering machine.

Shivering, I lie back down in bed and pull the heavy covers over my shoulders. I crave warmth. I lie staring up into the dark until just after seven, when a hint of light creeps in the window, light that is more like a shadow. Sliding one hand out from under the covers, I reach for the phone. Dial. Click. The familiar voice, the now relentless message.

I dial information to get the number for the Blue Moon. Then dial it on the off chance that someone is there, taking reservations or making preparations. Someone is. A woman answers.

"I'm not in town and I need to reach Gabriella," I say. "I've tried her at home several times and there's no answer. It's important."

"She's out of town." The woman's voice is young, bright. I can feel the warmth of the tropics in it.

"Do you know how I can reach her?"

"No. She's in the Bahamas."

The Bahamas. Did Gaby mention anything about going to the Bahamas? No, I am sure she didn't. "Is everything okay there?"

"Everything's just fine." I can practically see the smile on the face of the woman speaking to me as I huddle under my blankets.

"Know when she'll be back?"

"She stole away for a couple of days with her fiancé. I'm not really certain when she returns."

"Roy," I say.

"Yes."

"I see." For the first time I am suddenly alarmed. Perhaps it is the dream, but I am now afraid for Gaby's life. There is nothing I can do from here. And probably little that I can do there, but I know I have to go back to Key West. Today.

A dense fog hangs like a veil over the valley. So dense that I can see little more than ten feet in front of me when I walk to the café at seven-thirty, huddled in my canvas coat. It is wet and cold. Cars come out of the fog like apparitions, their windshield wipers on, their headlights like yellow cat's eyes.

At the café I find Don Cameron seated at the counter. He lifts a hand casually in greeting when I sit next to him.

"I've got reservations back to Florida today."

Don nods. "Something come up?"

I tell him.

"The Bahamas," he says, looking off into the distance. "Heard of it. Where is it?"

"A string of islands in the Atlantic not far off the coast of south Florida."

"Another resort, vacation place?"

"Yeah, exactly."

Don picks up his fork and mixes some egg with his hash browns. It is the same breakfast he ate yesterday, probably the one that he eats every day. Routine—an ordered life. Not, I realize, unlike my own life in Key West.

"When's your flight?"

"Ten o'clock."

Don checks his watch. "I'll drive you to the airport."

The fog has not lifted. After breakfast I walk back to

the hotel, put my meager things together, and check out. At eight-forty-five Don is out front in the Jeep and I begin my trip home. Driving slowly as we creep through the fog, Don says little until we get to the airport, when he wishes me luck. "I wish I could be there," he says. "I've got a stake in this."

We shake hands. "I'll keep you posted," I say.

The Tetons are invisible, their majesty shrouded in fog as we take off. Is the menace they impose on nervous fliers more acute when the mountains are seen, or not seen? It quickly becomes a moot question. At a thousand feet we break through the fog, pushing the trailing clouds aside, like a submarine suddenly surfacing from the dark depths of the sea; and there, in all their resplendent glory, are the snowcapped peaks bathed in bright sunlight. My grip on the armrest loosens and I begin to breathe easier.

Unlike the journey out here, the flights back are uneventful, and I even manage to sleep a good part of the way. I am due to arrive back in Key West at ten o'clock tonight, and though it has been just three days since I left, it feels like weeks. I begin to make plans for my return. The sea beckons. I promise myself a swim first thing tomorrow morning. A kind of baptism.

And, hanging in the balance, is Gaby. Surely, someone in the Blue Moon will know exactly where she can be reached in the Bahamas, so that I can at least phone her. The woman whom I spoke to earlier this morning said that she was stealing a couple of days. Gaby may even be back by tomorrow. Unless—

I put the thought out of my mind.

After a delayed flight out of Orlando it is closer to midnight when I reach Key West. Stepping off the plane, I breathe in the familiar scent, the sea smell mixed with that of the cloying, but less familiar, aviation fuel. The air is damp, but warm, the costly canvas coat that had been such a comfort only a few hours ago, now a burden—uncomfortably irritating against my bare arm over which it hangs as I make my way into the terminal.

Taxicabs line the roadway in front of the terminal, and beyond toward the beach, I can see the shadows of the tall, stately palm trees, leaning leeward, their dark fronds stirring in the light late-night breeze. Swept along the boulevard by taxi, the windows down, jazz spilling out into the night from the radio, I am home.

When the cab stops on Duval Street, I am suddenly reminded of what I have returned to. The shambles of the *groceria* stands like a desecrated shrine, soot-blackened.

In three days, however, my own place has been transformed. Freshly painted, it is like new. The carpenter has removed his tools, cleaned up the mess, and, in a phrase, I am back in business.

The only message on the answering machine is from Frank Pappagallo. When it has played and the machine clicks off, I hear a scratching sound that seems to come from the kitchen. I walk back there, turn the light on, and listen. And hear it again, something scratching against the back door. Turning the porch light on, I open the door. Tom, my cat is there, his front paw lifted. I have not seen him since the fire, but I left water and food dishes out and instructed the carpenter to fill them each day.

His coat is smudged, and Tom seems thinner, more unstable when he stands, yawns, and hobbles inside, purring once as he wends through my legs.

I dump the water that is in his bowl into the sink and refill it. Tom drinks when I set it on the floor. There is nothing in the refrigerator for him, but I put a few cans of cat food on the shelf before I left and see that they are still there, suggesting that this must be his first time home since the fire. Old and blind in one eye, he would have had a hard time fending for himself, but I assume that he has managed to find scraps in the neighborhood, maybe a lizard or two to keep him going.

He sniffs at the canned food I put down. Then settles on his haunches to eat, slowly and deliberately, his one good eye closed. Tom eats less than half of what I put out for him before sitting back, running a paw over his face, then looking up at me. I scratch him between the ears. Then follow him into the office, where he struggles to clamber inside the file drawer in my desk.

It is after one o'clock by the time I shower, make up my bed, and turn in, falling asleep under a crisp sheet with the overhead fan stirring the air, the cold of Wyoming now only a distant memory.

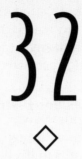

32

◇

Pop is the first person I see the next morning. He and his son, Orlando, are clearing the debris from the ruined store, wearing gloves as they pick up the burnt wood, piece by piece, and toss it into the back of a truck parked behind the *groceria*.

"Oh, you come back, Bud," Pop says when I walk over to where they are working.

Is there some coolness in Pop's tone of voice, or is it my imagination? He does not stop working.

"I got back late last night," I tell him.

"They finish your place. Everything is fine."

"Yes. What about you? What are you going to do?"

Pop pauses, a charred two-by-four in his hand. He stares at me. "We going to sell, Bud."

We look at each other, and everything in that look speaks volumes, more than words will convey. And with it, I seem to make my own decision. I will not linger here, to be built around, surrounded, becoming a kind of dinosaur frozen in time. I, too, will sell. Pop picks up the wood, cradling it in both hands, before giving me a final look, then flinging part of his life into the truck bed.

In the drugstore, half a dozen people sit at a table, their faces painted. Some in half masks with feathers crowning their heads. I am reminded that it is almost Halloween, Fantasy Fest. And although the parade is still a couple of days away, the revelry seems to have begun.

Frank Pappagallo is at the counter, and I sit next to him.

"Bud, where the hell you been?" Frank asks.

"Out of town."

"Since when did you become a travelin' man?"

"It was work, Frank."

I put my order in with Mary the waitress as the revelers file out, dancing in a sort of conga line, and blowing on paper noisemakers that curl away from their lips like snakes.

"Let the good times roll," Frank says.

"Pop tells me he's selling," I remark when they are gone.

"That's what I was calling to tell you."

"What kind of a price did he get?"

Frank looks away, his mouth arching downward. "Below market." He pauses a beat, then adds, "Way below. But he hasn't got much choice. What's he going to do, rebuild?"

Inwardly, I wince, but something in my expression must show because Frank says, "I'm sorry, Bud." The way he says it, I am unsure if he is apologizing for himself, or me.

"Have they linked anyone to the fire?"

Frank shakes his head. "They think it was some crack addicts. They found a Coke can with holes in it like they use to smoke that shit."

"I don't believe it."

"Why not?"

"One, my bedroom wall's ten yards from the *groceria*. I'm a light sleeper. I've been awakened before by kids smoking back there."

"Maybe you were sleeping hard, Bud."

"Two, that fire was too intense in a very short time. It had to be fueled by something more than a spark from a crack pipe."

"The investigators found some evidence of oily rags and a can of linseed oil in what had been a storage closet where Pop kept his cleaning supplies. They think that's what fueled it."

"Maybe," I reply, looking away.

"You still think this was deliberate, Bud? That someone burned Pop out to get him to sell? I don't think you're going to get too far with that anymore."

"We'll see."

"Bud, I wouldn't start a vendetta, pushing peoples' noses out of joint."

"You keep warning me about that, Frank. If it was just a couple of crack addicts, what are you afraid of?"

Frank shakes his head. "Oh, what the hell. Sometimes there's no reasoning with you, Bud."

When Mary puts my breakfast down, Frank returns to his paper and I eat in silence. "What do you hear about Gaby?" I ask when I am finished.

"Not a thing. Why?"

"Apparently, she's over in the Bahamas with Roy Emerson."

"So? She's taking a vacation. No crime in that, is there?"

I pick up my check. "I hope not."

"What's that supposed to mean?"

"Exactly what I said. I hope there isn't any crime."

"Sometimes, Bud, I just don't understand you."

"I wouldn't lie awake nights trying," I reply, standing up from the counter.

"Wait a minute, Bud. What about you?"

"What about me?"

"You come to any decisions on your place?"

"I have," I say. "I'm ready to sell."

Frank beams. "No kidding."

"I'm not kidding. The place is on the market. You're the first to know, Frank."

"You got a figure in mind?"

"As a matter of fact, I do."

"Well?"

"Market value plus whatever loss Pop was forced to take on his deal."

Frank's face drops.

"Handle it for me, Frank. I'm counting on you." Taking my check to the register, I pay, then give the crestfallen Frank Pappagallo a wave on the way out.

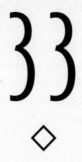

33

◇

After breakfast, I put on a pair of swim trunks and carry a towel and mask three blocks down to the beach at the end of Duval. The water is cool and clear as glass. Wading out to waist-deep water, I adjust the mask on my head, then plunge in, feeling the skin-tightening tingle of salt, bracing as I begin my mile-long swim. An hour later, my muscles loosened up after the days of cold and tension, I return home and stand under a long cool shower.

The rest of the morning I spend on the phone trying unsuccessfully to track down Gaby. She seems to have vanished; yes, to the Bahamas, but no one apparently knows where exactly in the Bahamas, or for how long she will be gone. Everyone I talk to agrees that it is very unlike Gaby, who is normally so punctilious, so methodical. "You could set your watch by her," one of her friends tells me. Very mysterious.

She seemed okay when she left, I am told. Nothing unusual about her. Happy. Glad to be getting off the rock for a while.

I pursue my questioning trying not to sound an alarm, for it is certain that when she returns, Gaby will hear from a variety of people that I have been asking about her.

At noon I decide to call and leave a message on her answering machine. The phone rings three times, during which I prepare my spiel, ready to deliver it when the machine clicks on. But it doesn't. Instead, the phone is answered on the fourth ring by a breathless Gaby. "Bud!" she says. "When did you get back?"

"Last night. Late. How about you?"

"This morning. Less than an hour ago, in fact."

"You didn't tell me you were going away."

"It was kind of spur-of-the-moment."

"Where'd you go?"

"Bimini."

"Good time?"

"The best."

"Just you and Roy?"

"*Hmm uh.* Bud, you've got your investigator's tone of voice. Is anything wrong?"

"Nope. Curious is all. Sort of unusual for you take off like that, isn't it?"

"Not when you're getting married."

"What?"

"Are you going deaf, Bud? I said, not when you're getting married."

"I heard you. I was surprised. I didn't think you were going to do it this soon."

"Changed our minds. We didn't want a big to-do. So we just decided to elope and get it over with."

"Your idea?"

"Mostly Roy's, but I wasn't against it."

"Let me be the first to congratulate you."

Gaby laughs. "Thanks, Bud. Now tell me about your trip."

"I probably ought to wait on that," I say. "Is Roy moving into your place?"

"Because of his work we're going to keep the same arrangement for the time being. He'll spend weekends out here."

"So the marriage was just a piece of paper. A formality."

"Bud, that sounds terribly cold. What's wrong with you?"

"Are you happy?"

"Very."

"Can I still see you? I mean for dinner sometime. Just the two of us."

Gaby tries to laugh again, but it is not quite so carefree. "Of course you can, Bud. Anytime. Nothing's changed."

"How about this evening?"

Gaby hesitates. "I suppose. I hadn't really intended to go back to work until tomorrow."

"And Roy?"

"What about him?"

"He won't mind?"

"Bud, what's gotten into you? Is something wrong?"

"I need to talk to you."

"You can talk to me anytime. Nothing's changed between us just because I'm married."

"I'm glad to hear that."

"Would you like to go to the Blue Moon?"

"How about someplace off the beaten track? In your area maybe."

"All right. There are a couple of places nearby. Why don't you drive up around seven and we'll go together?"

"Perfect. I'll see you at seven."

Have I pushed too hard, sounding some alarm in Gaby? I wonder. The trick is going to be to make her wary without completely warning her that she may be married to a murderer. I do not know how to do that. Her marriage to Roy has made the situation even more delicate now. And, if the past can be any indication of things to come, time will not be on our side. I must take some decisive action but without alienating Gaby.

After hanging up, I call Fred Pacey's office.

"Mr. Pacey's in a meeting right now," his secretary tells me. "Can I take a message?"

" 'May.' "

"What?"

" 'May I take a message.' "

"I'm sorry, I don't—"

"Forget about it. What time do you expect he will be free?"

"I really don't know." Whatever warmth her voice contained has evaporated.

"I'll check back later."

"He'll be going to lunch after his meeting ends, and I don't expect him back the rest of the day."

"Thanks. I'll catch up with him."

With the thousand-dollar check from Bob Hargreaves in my pocket, I bike down to the bank, which is directly across the street from Fred Pacey's office building. After depositing the check, I pick up a newspaper and stand at one of several counters for filling out deposit slips, one that is near a window and affords a view across the street.

Twenty minutes later, Fred Pacey comes out of his office. He is accompanied by Frank Pappagallo. And Roy Faulkner Emerson.

34

◇

Fortunately, the trio remains on foot, easy enough to follow. A crowd of tourists prowl the streets with blank expressions, gawking at the gift shops, refreshment stands, bars, and restaurants, and I quickly blend in amongst them.

A couple of blocks from his office, Pacey and his party turn into one of the restaurants, an outdoor joint where a deck has been built around the spreading limbs of an old banyan tree on the second floor. I watch from the sidewalk below as they are seated at one of the tables overlooking the street.

Across the street is a square where outdoor vendors sell jewelry and trinkets from their mobile carts. There are some park benches in the shade of another banyan tree. Also beneath it a Filipino guy, wearing a hand-made hat woven from thin strips of palm fronds, sits on the padded bicycle seat attached to his pushcart containing cold drinks. He is working a crossword puzzle folded from the morning newspaper, occasionally touching the tip of his lead pencil against his tongue before writing in a word.

Crossing the street, I enter the square and approach him. "Elmore. How's business?"

Elmore looks up. He wears glasses with lenses a quarter of an inch thick, magnifying his already big brown eyes. He grins; his large teeth flashing in his pink gums are flat white, like old ivory piano keys. "Cain't complain, Bud. Always a buck to make round chere."

Elmore is from the Philippines, a World War II refugee. He has somehow made a living plying the tourist trade. "Selling ice tea today?"

"Sure, why not?" Elmore puts his paper on a shelf attached to his cart, weighing it down with a conch shell, and takes a paper cup with the Coca-Cola logo from a stack, fills it with shaved ice from one compartment; then taking out a gallon jug of tea from another compartment, he pours the tea into the cup. "Want some key lime, Bud?"

I nod, watching as he squeezes juice from half a lime into the tea. "How much, Elmore?"

"Three bits." Elmore learned his English from American GIs in the Philippines.

I give him a dollar and tell him to keep the change.

"Thanks, Bud. Maria got some hot bollos and conch fritters down the way."

Looking in the direction he points, I see Elmore's wife at another stand, and walk over there to get half a dozen of the wok-fried fritters before going to a bench in the shade of the banyan, where I can eat while still being able to observe Pacey having lunch with Frank and Roy on the restaurant deck in the distance.

The fritters are perfect, spicy, plenty of garlic, light on the inside with a crispy exterior. Probably not what Doc Russell would recommend, but otherwise I have been diligent about the diet. An occasional reward seems harmless enough. The iced tea tastes freshly brewed. A light breeze drifts through the heavy-branched tree as a young black kid begins working on a set of steel drums at the opposite end of the square.

Half an hour goes by as I watch tourists mill around, haggling with the vendors over the price of costume jewelry. Then, an hour after they went into the restaurant, Pacey and company depart, retracing their footsteps. Pacey goes back to the office, and Roy and Frank stand outside talking for a few minutes before going off in different directions.

Frank turns onto Duval Street, ambling along leisurely, pausing now and then to look into shop windows. Everywhere Halloween festoons the atmosphere. Cheap paper cutouts of hobgoblins and vampires dripping bloody teeth cavort together in windows streaming with fuzzy gauzelike cotton candy, while jack-o'-lanterns seem to pucker and wilt under the tropical climate.

"Clever, isn't it, Frank?" I ask. He has stopped in front of a department store window, staring at a witch on a broomstick attached to a hidden track in the ceiling and flying around the interior perimeter. Once every revolution a tinny cackle emits from a loudspeaker. "Who would have thought Key West would ever get this kind of big-city sophistication. I remember when the best we could do for a holiday was a skinny Santa Claus in a moth-eaten red suit in the Christmas parade."

"Earl Tidwell," Frank says, continuing to stare at the witch.

"What?"

"Earl Tidwell. He was always the Santa. After Webb Conners put on so much weight, they tried to get him one year, but Earl wouldn't stand for it. Tradition, he told the city. Tucked a pillow up under his suit and went on until he died. Probably the oldest Santa in the country."

"I didn't know that."

"Times change, Bud."

"Sure they do. How was your lunch?"

Frank looks startled for a moment, then laughs. "You get around, don't you, Bud?"

"Now and then. Tell me about Roy Emerson."

"What do you want to know?"

"What he's got going with Fred Pacey?"

"He's handling the details on the upper Duval development."

"My place?"

Frank nods.

"You told them about my offer?"

"Of course, Bud."

"What did Pacey say?"

"He wasn't happy."

"He wasn't happy. That's all?"

"He didn't say no."

"And he didn't say yes."

Frank glances back at the witch.

"Maybe I better stay awake nights from now on," I say.

◇

How well do you know Roy?"

Wearing a linen jacket over a blouse whose collar is turned up around her neck, Gaby gazes at me across the table in the outdoor restaurant a couple of miles from her home. A quizzical expression centers on her face. "I'm not sure what you're getting at, Bud. How well does anyone know anyone?"

"What I mean is, his background, his past." I realize I am stumbling, on shaky ground here. "His people," I add.

"Bud Lowry, are you jealous?" Gaby lifts her wineglass, smiling. I can't help but notice the diamond that glints on her ring finger.

Forcing a smile of my own, I lift my glass, touching hers. "Curious."

"One of the things I love about you, Bud, is your protectiveness. You're so insulated. It's really—" She seems to search for a word.

"Quaint."

"Sort of."

"I never thought of myself in those terms."

"Well, you know what I mean. I talked to friends today who said you'd called them. Are you worried about me? What's going on, Bud?"

A waitress comes and takes our order, giving me a brief respite. A chance to regroup.

But Gaby doesn't give me the opportunity. She bores in. "You still don't like Roy, do you? You think I've made a mistake."

"He's involved with Fred Pacey and the development project in my block. Did you know that?"

Gaby nods. "So," she says with some finality, "that's it."

"I can't say I'm exactly happy about it."

Gaby is sympathetic. "I understand. I'm sure I'd feel the same way. But you've got to separate Roy my husband from Roy the guy whose work you don't like. Or maybe you don't have to, but I do."

"Sure. I wish it was that easy."

"It has to be that easy, Bud. Otherwise our relationship is compromised. Yours and mine. And I don't want that to happen. We've always been very close."

Almost like lovers, I think, we stare into one another's eyes. "I don't want that to happen, either," I say.

"Then you've got to give Roy and me a chance. If you've got to fight with him, fine. I will understand. But please leave me out of it." She picks up her glass and drinks.

"Just one personal question?"

"Of course."

"Are you investing in this deal?"

"Bud, you're incorrigible. No."

But she does shift in her seat, I notice, crossing her legs beneath the table. She squirms.

I change the subject. "Nice rock," I say, admiring the ring. "Looks expensive."

With her thumb Gaby pushes the ring around on her finger. "It is a family heirloom," she says. "It belonged to Roy's grandmother."

Heirloom! The sonofabitch hasn't even paid for her ring! He could have told Gaby anything. It may even have belonged to his first wife, Karen. I make a mental note to call and ask Bob Hargreaves what became of his daughter's engagement ring.

I lift my glass once again in a toast. "Good luck, Gaby."

"Thanks. What are you thinking about?"

"Nothing." But I can see that Gaby doesn't believe me. Someone else crossed my mind just now, another marriage.

"Bud, is everything okay?"

"Fine."

Our food arrives. For a moment it is like old times. Gaby savors each bite, delineating each flavor, while providing a running commentary. By her standards, it isn't that good. An overuse of fruit to add flavor to over-cooked fish. My lamb with mint sauce fares better. Nothing unusual, but there's something to be said for tradition, Gaby says. Then for a time we eat in silence.

"What about the trip you took?" Gaby asks, over coffee. "Tell me about it?"

"A case I'm working on," I say. "I can't really talk about it."

"Not even where you were."

I shake my head. "The West Coast." Knowing she will think Florida's west coast, that I would never have ventured all the way to the other side of the country. And, of course, had it not been for her, I would not have.

"Sometimes I think that you're being deliberately mysterious."

"And sometimes I have to be."

"And I have the feeling that it has to do with Roy."

The waitress brings the check. Gaby and I both reach for it. "On me this time," I say.

"Well, does it?" she asks, relinquishing her hold on the check.

"Does what?"

"Have anything to do with Roy?"

I smile. "Suppose I told you Roy was a serial killer?"

Gaby laughs. "I wouldn't believe you."

"Then it wouldn't make sense to tell you, would it?"

"But it isn't that bad, so tell me the truth."

I shrug. "Come on, Gaby. Let's get out of here."

We both stand up. I sense her nervousness. Perhaps I have done the right thing, having at least cautioned her without putting her in a position of denial, of having to defend Roy. I don't know.

We have come in Gaby's car, and we drive back to her place in silence. A cloud seems to have fallen over us, both of us tense, as if we are unsure how to proceed. As for myself, I now know what I have to do. Gaby's survival may depend on how well I do it.

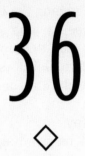

36

◇

Gaby has told me that Roy Emerson lives in a condominium on the beach, and at seven-thirty the next morning I park the Buick on a side street where I am able to see both driveways leading in and out of the building.

With its toneless gray bulk that is monstrously out of proportion with the neighborhood, the condo is an eyesore that no amount of landscaping can hide. The puttylike walls and small flat windows of each of the twin wings resemble nothing so much as those of a prison. And by blocking the tolerant easterly sea breezes from reaching those of us inland, it has, in a sense, made prisoners of us all.

A few minutes before eight I see Roy drive out in his sports car. Leaving the Buick where it is, I walk across the street to one of the two entrances, where the building directory is located. One R. Emerson is listed in apartment 308 G. Pushing the intercom button next to his name, I hear a beep, which goes unanswered.

Locked glass doors lead to the interior of the building, where there are two elevators. A young couple is just coming out of one elevator, and I stand at the door, smiling as they exit.

"Forgot my key," I say.

The guy holds the door, grinning, but without paying much attention to me as he keeps up a conversation with his companion. I ride the elevator up to the third floor and exit onto a long, depressing corridor with apartment doors on either side of it. Overhead spotlighting casts weird shadows as I advance along the corridor, which seems to go on for half a mile, my soft-soled shoes squeaking against the tiles.

At the far end is 308 G, the last door, in fact. Roy no doubt has an apartment with a sea view. Each door has a peephole, and there is no way my approach could have gone unmonitored if someone were on the other side of the door.

Further back down the hallway, a door opens and closes, and as I knock lightly on Roy's door, I glance back quickly to see a man beginning his long march to the elevators. After a few seconds I try the door, which is, as I was sure it would be, locked.

The only keyhole is in the doorknob, which means, luckily, that there is no deadbolt. Certainly, a considerable savings to the developer with the number of doors in this place.

Satisfied that I've got the information I came for, I turn and walk back to the elevators, sure that on my next visit I won't have any problem picking the lock.

Back home, I call Fred Pacey's office and am told that

he is not expected in before ten. Do I want to leave a message?

No, I don't. I want a cup of coffee and to read the paper, which I didn't have time for this morning, so I head over by bike to the drugstore and make good on one wish, anyway.

By a quarter to ten I am at Fred Pacey's building, lingering outside, waiting for the great man himself. He does not disappoint. At five past ten he strolls around the corner, his brow knit, but that could just have been from the too tightly knotted tie at his throat.

"Morning, Fred."

Pacey looks up. He has the startled but resolute stare of a small animal that has been captured in the glare of headlights. His hair seems to have thinned more since we last met, and his face has the sallow, pasty complexion of someone who spends too much time under fluorescent lighting.

The last time we met was under unfavorable circumstances, and I can see in Pacey's eyes the dawning awareness that this is not a coincidental meeting; I spell trouble. He looks at his watch.

"I've got a busy morning, Bud. I'm already late for an appointment."

"I'm not going to take up much time," I say.

Pacey seems to hesitate, as if he is unsure whether to barge past me or listen to what I have to say. Curiosity wins out. "What is it, Bud?"

Smiling, I tell him. I tell him what I think of his planned destruction of my neighborhood. I tell him what I think of his attempt to capitalize on the misfortune of my friend Pop. I put a little touch of sarcasm in my voice when I pronounce "misfortune" so that there is no uncertainty in regard to my feelings about that event.

Passersby, tourists, pause, looking at us. Pacey turns a shade darker in the face, running a finger between his neck and collar, a grimace on his otherwise expressionless face. I give him the clincher.

"Twenty-four hours," I say. "To make a decision on my offer. After that the price goes up, or I may even withdraw the offer altogether."

Pacey squares his shoulders. "Is that it, Bud?"

"No." I lift the end of his tie, rubbing my thumb against the silk. "Nice. Expensive." Then let it drop. "Any accidents, the sort of misfortune that occurred to Pop—I rebuild." I get on my bike. "That's it, Fred. Have a nice day."

I am home less than an hour when the phone rings. It is Frank.

"Bud, what the hell are you doing?"

"Making a point."

"Fred is furious."

"Good. For a while I was afraid he had no emotions."

"I wouldn't push him."

"He pushed me and I'm pushing back. That's what it comes down to."

"He's got a lot of influence in this town."

"With arsonists?"

"Bud, you're on shaky ground there."

"I wonder where I might find Roy Emerson this time of day."

"What do you want with him?"

"I'd just feel a little more secure if I knew where he was."

◇

Roy doesn't have an office, Frank tells me. He works out of other people's offices. Or, Frank confides, when he can, out of his car.

"What do you mean 'out of his car'?"

Frank laughs. "Roy's one of those guys who likes to be on the move. Can't seem to sit still for long. Likes to do business on the road, working the cellular. He'll think nothing of driving eighty or a hundred miles up the Keys to take someone to lunch, or dinner."

"He must be doing business with people who've got a lot of time on their hands."

"When he's trying to nail down a contract, I guess it's impressive. Roy's smooth."

"So I hear. Are you impressed, Frank?"

"Bud, between you and me, I don't like the guy. Okay? There's something about him, and I can't tell you what it is, but I don't like him. But I'll tell you something else. I'm not going to cross him, either."

"Level with me, Frank. Do you think he started that fire?"

"No. Now, do you want to ask me do I think he could have had a hand in someone else starting it? I'd say yes, it's possible. But I'd only say that to you, Bud, and you repeat it, I'll deny it."

"What about Gabriella?"

"What about her?"

"She married him."

"Listen, Bud, I'm a lawyer. Not a shrink. What brings two people together is beyond me. You ask me, half the married people I know, it doesn't make sense. But that's their business. As a lawyer, all I've got to do is get them out of it when it's time. Not analyze it."

In the street outside, a car painted orange and black drives by, a huge carved pumpkin with flashing lights mounted on its roof. A ghost is driving. Frank warns me once again against pushing Fred Pacey.

"Frank, I want this settled. I gave him twenty-four hours, and I meant it."

Frank sighs. "Bud, take my advice. Do what the kids today say."

"What's that?"

"Chill."

"I don't like the cold."

Frank does not laugh. "If you sell, have you thought about what you're going to do? Where you'll live?"

"Maybe I'll just rent a place."

"As your lawyer, I wouldn't advise you to do that. You sell this place and don't invest it, the capital gains taxes will kill you. "

"So as my lawyer, what would you advise me to do?"

"Buy something."

"You got any leads?"

"As a matter of fact. While you were away, Bud, your place on William Street went on the market."

I feel a tightening in my chest. "My place."

"The ancestral home. Where you grew up."

Images of my childhood play before me. "It's a big house," I say. It had been converted to a bed and breakfast a decade or so ago.

"Not that big. You could live in the downstairs, have your office there, and rent out the upstairs. Have some income out of it."

I have not been in the place in nearly twenty-five years, but my mind has often been haunted by memories of my life there with my father, Captain Billy, my mother, Phyllis, and my brother, Carl, all of whom are dead. "What are they asking?"

"I think you could get it for under five."

I know that he means $500,000. And I also know that my mother could never have imagined the place would be worth that kind of money only twenty-five years after her death. "Where am I going to get that kind of money, Frank?"

"Have you forgotten what you're asking for your place? You make a sizable down payment, with money left over to make whatever changes you need to make to get some rental income. You'll be in a quiet neighborhood, off Duval Street, sitting pretty. What do you think?"

I think it sounds crazy. "When can I look at it?" I ask.

"I could set something up this afternoon."

We agree on a time, and when we hang up, I call Gaby, reaching her at home.

"I apologize," I say when she answers.

"For?"

"I had no business questioning your judgment. I was out of line. I truly hope you'll be happy."

"Thanks, Bud. I confess I've been bothered by our conversation."

"Forget it. You're special, Gaby. Maybe I am jealous."

"Don't be. You know how I feel about you, Bud."

"Have you seen Roy?"

"No, but he'll be here this evening."

"I'd just as soon you didn't say anything to him about last night."

"I hadn't planned on it."

"Maybe we can get together again. I'll be better behaved."

"Of course, Bud. Anytime."

Before hanging up, I tell her about my plan to look at the old Lowry homestead.

"That's wonderful," Gaby says. "Do it. It would be a kind of homecoming."

I am not so sure. But for whatever reasons, I have agreed to at least look at the house, and I find that it has provoked a strange nervousness in me, the sort of feeling that comes with the thought of impending confrontation.

38

◇

At two o'clock I am on William Street, standing beneath the familiar royal poinciana tree, whose barren sticklike branches poke through the tangle of electrical wires stretched between wooden poles along the street. At this time of year it is always difficult to imagine these brittle, flaky trees exploding in fiery orange blossoms each spring, but in my childhood I awaited their arrival with the keen awareness that the first stab of color heralded the end of school and the approaching summer.

The exterior of the frame house is gray with green trim and shutters, the wide front porch bedecked with white wrought-iron porch furniture. It is inviting, welcoming. Everything clean, cool, and protected in the shade of the sheltering palm trees that grow on either side of the old poinciana.

"Looks pretty good, doesn't it, Bud?"

Soundlessly, catching me by surprise, Frank has come up beside me.

"A little more gussied up than it ever was when I was growing up here."

"You'll be able to tone it down once you're living in it."

"You seem confident I'm going to buy it."

"It makes sense," Frank says. "Come on. I've got the key."

I follow Frank up the sidewalk and watch as he unlocks the door to a place I have not been inside in nearly twenty-five years, since my mother's death.

The layout remains essentially unchanged from the way I remember it. Two front bedrooms off either side of the long hallway, with a stairway leading to the second floor, where there are two more bedrooms and a bath. In the back is the large kitchen and screened-in porch looking out over the deck under the shade of the thick, green leaves of a giant sapodilla tree.

Frank leads me through as if he's conducting a tour. "My idea," he says, "is one of the front bedrooms you could use, the other you'd turn into your office. Upstairs you put in a kitchenette and you've got a ready-made rental apartment. The place isn't that big, but it gives you some space, and everything is in good condition. That way it will generate income that should pay for whatever modest mortgage you have to carry."

Frank seems to have it all figured out. It's true. The hardwood floors have been kept up, everything is painted and clean. As a kid the place did seem much bigger. Now it is just a house, and I am happy not to be overwhelmed with the ghosts of my past.

"Well, what do you think?" Frank asks. We are standing in the kitchen. Everything is in place, but it is clear no one is living here. The cabinets are empty. There is nothing in the fridge.

"Why is it on the market?"

"Two guys operated it as a guesthouse. One of them died of AIDS a few months ago. His partner kept the business going for a while, but he just didn't have the enthusiasm for operating the place alone. He gave it up a month ago and left town."

An all too familiar story.

"To get a quick turnover, he's ready to make the price attractive."

"And what would that be?"

"I checked at the realty company. Four twenty-five."

I scoff. "Captain Billy bought the place for less than a thousand dollars."

"Sure. And twenty-five years ago you could hardly give one of these places away."

I try to remember what my brother and I sold the place for after Phyllis died. Maybe a hundred thousand.

"What I'm saying," Frank says, "is you're making an investment here. You sell your place, and put the money in this. You can't lose."

"If I get the price I'm asking for my place."

"I talked to Fred before I came over here. He's going to make an offer."

"I made the offer. All he's got to do is accept it. I made that plain."

"Okay. Okay." Frank looks skyward, exasperated. "Just hear what he has to say. I don't know what he's going to do. He didn't tell me."

Bob Hargreaves flashes across my mind, he and his wife Ruth, still living in the house his grandfather had homesteaded.

"I'll keep it in mind," I tell Frank.

He nods, but appears unconvinced. "I'm looking out for your best interests. This would be a good deal for you, Bud."

"I said I'll think about it."

Frank shrugs, and we leave the house, Frank locking the door. After telling him I will be in touch, I get on my bike and head home.

The space I have been living in the past thirty years seems spartan after revisiting the house where I grew up. Maybe Frank is right, it would make sense, but I wonder if I could adjust. If I am prepared to handle the intrusion of the past at this time in my life.

As I consider it all, the phone rings. It is Roy Emerson. From the background noise I can tell that he is on his cellular phone, in his car. "Bud, this is Roy. Gaby's husband."

I can hear what sounds like a smirk in his voice.

"I think we should talk," he continues. "Float some ideas around."

"What kind of ideas?"

Roy laughs. "The only kind that matter. Numbers."

"And when would you like to float these numbers?"

"How about tomorrow morning? I'll be up at Gaby's tonight, but I could drive in and pick you up at ten. Maybe have lunch up the Keys."

That would be fine, I tell him. And perhaps, after the work I intend to do tonight, we'll even have something more interesting to talk about than numbers.

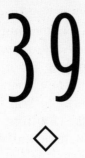

39

◇

The building where Roy lives is more imposing and sinister in the dark than it is in daylight. At eight-thirty I park in the dimly lit lot. Wearing a dark sport jacket and an old straw hat I found in my closet, I walk up to the glass entry door where I was allowed in this morning. It is quiet, no one around. As a precaution, I punch in Roy's number and, as expected, get no answer.

When a car drives into the parking lot, I walk away from the building, listening as a man's footsteps walk across the drive and up to the entrance. Hearing the door click, I turn and walk back, lingering in the shadows of shrubbery where I can watch the door. If I can get in the condo as someone is leaving rather than entering, I figure my chances of being seen and remembered will be reduced in the event something goes amiss.

It's the dinner hour for people who live in fancy condos on the water, the time, I've calculated, when there should be the least movement in and out. Fifteen minutes pass before anyone comes out.

As two women leave the elevator together, I walk toward the door, fumbling for my keys, timing it so that I get there just as they open the door. It goes as smoothly as the earlier rehearsal. The women seem to pay no attention to me. Smiling, I hold the door for them, then go in and take the waiting elevator. On the ride up I take from my jacket pocket the two lock picks I've brought with me, palming them as the elevator door opens on the third floor. A middle-aged guy is waiting. He steps back to let me out. We speak, and as he enters the elevator, I begin the long march down the corridor.

Although the lock on Roy's door is as easy to pick as I anticipated it would be, twice I am forced to step aside and hide in a narrow alcove beside the fire extinguisher when I hear the elevator or people entering or exiting their apartments.

Finally, when the corridor is clear the second time, I go back to Roy's door and, with just the right pressure, feel the tumblers fall into place as the knob turns in my hand.

Stepping inside and closing the door behind me, I stand for several seconds letting my eyes adjust to the dark. A hallway gives onto a kitchen and, beyond that, the living room. A quick walk-through reveals a two-bedroom, one-bath apartment. Everything is furnished in the standard, homogenous furnishings one would expect in a luxury rental unit. A sofa, a glass-topped coffee table, a couple of matching leather chairs, and a dining room with a bamboo-and-glass table and four bamboo chairs covered in some sort of tropical print. The kitchen has all the modern conveniences. Dishwasher, garbage disposal, and a freezer with an ice dispenser. In the fridge, I find a bottle of V-8 juice, a half-empty container of milk, three eggs, and an unopened package of cheddar cheese. Everything is neatly ordered, in its place, as if no one lives here or, more probably, I think, Roy is the type to have a maid come in on a routine basis.

In the living room two long, narrow, fixed windows, incapable of being opened, look out over the beach. Between them a door opens onto a small balcony. Along an adjacent wall is a new desk, designed, however, to look as though it were an antique. A small laptop computer is positioned in the center of the desk. Beside it is a telephone and answering machine, its red message light blinking insistently. I close the drapes over the windows, then switch on the brass desk lamp with its green shade and sit down behind the desk.

A few papers cover the desk's surface. Glancing at them, I see that one is an American Express bill, the others mostly advertising circulars and catalogs. I pick up the AmEx bill. The itemized list of charges suggests a spree in Miami in the past month. Restaurant charges, each meal totaling more than a hundred dollars. Nearly three hundred in charges at Bloomingdale's and over five hundred in a jewelry store in Coral Gables. All told, Roy has racked up more than two thousand dollars in expenses for the previous month on Am Ex, most of them from Miami, incurred in a matter of days.

Before turning to the answering machine, I jot down in my pocket notepad the names of the establishments Roy has frequented in Miami, as well as the dates of his consumption and purchases.

The answering machine looks like a quality, high-priced instrument, with automatic speed-dial and a variety of other buttons, along with a message screen and some features that mean nothing to me. I press the message button, confident that whatever is on the machine will not be erased.

A beep and Fred Pacey's voice comes on, asking Roy to call him first thing in the morning.

Another beep. And the sound of a receiver hanging up. Beep. "Hi, honey," a woman's voice says. Young. But not Gaby's. "Listen, my plans got changed. I'm going to be in all evening. So call me whenever you get this and let's talk. I'm bored." There is a flirtatious laugh before she hangs up. A beep followed by three beeps, and the machine clicks off.

For a while I sit staring at the phone. Roy has a mother who is alive, no other relatives that I know of, but this was not a mother's voice. Or a sister's. It had the unmistakably intimate tone of a lover, a girlfriend.

Opening the desk drawers, I search for an address book. Roy is extremely neat, organized. Everything labeled, put together in some order. Carefully trying not to disturb any of it, I examine the various bits and pieces of paper. Unable to find an address book, I walk into the bedroom and look on a bedside table, where there is another phone. No book. Nothing in the drawer of the table.

In the closet, Roy's clothes hang neatly, shirts together on one side, a few suits with nothing in their pockets, several pairs of shoes lined up and a couple pairs of cowboy boots, polished. I return to the desk in the living room.

A few first names, some initials have been penned next to the speed-dial buttons on the phone. Except for Gaby's name, the others mean nothing to me. The other names are men's. And there are a half-dozen listings with initials only. I pick up the phone, press the button next to an initial, listening to a ring that goes unanswered.

After disconnecting, I press a second button, and a man answers on the third ring. I hang up, then try a third button. Four rings and I am about to hang up when a woman answers.

"Hi, Roy, that was quick. I really didn't expect to hear from you tonight. Hang on, a sec, I just got out of the shower. I'm standing here dripping wet."

I stand there mesmerized. It is the same voice I heard on the answering machine. She must have caller ID, which means when she next talks to Roy, he will know someone has been in the apartment. I hang up. And wonder what I should do? I can call back with some lame excuse, but I am damned if I can think of one that would prevent her from saying anything to Roy. I am pondering that when the phone rings. I stare at it. A little light has come on the message screen with the name Page Anderson and a phone number.

The answering machine takes the call, and Page says, "Roy, what's going on? Are you playing games with me? You just called. Pick up the phone. Come on, honey. Don't do this. Roy . . . Roy? Come on, pick up the phone. I know you're there. . . . All right. You'll never know what you missed." That flirtatious laughter. Then, click. She hangs up.

40

◇

Page Anderson. After calling information in a couple of places in the 305 area code, I find her listed in Coral Gables. A Miami residential district. It is now ten past nine. I have been in Roy's apartment less than an hour, but in that time I seem to have uncovered an interesting little side piece to his life story. Perhaps there is a perfectly reasonable explanation of it; nothing more than an old family friend. And perhaps, as we used to say, the moon is made of green cheese.

I consider my options. Whether to call Page again and confront her with the truth, that Roy Emerson is a married man, or to confront Roy. Either way I need to quiz her, to find out what his exact relationship with her is, and I cannot risk revealing my identity. Roy is soon going to know that someone called Page from his apartment, and that should no doubt sound an alarm with him. I decide to call her tonight from a pay phone, even though there is no reason for Roy to connect me to the break-in.

Before leaving, I turn off the light, open the drapes, then go through the apartment to be sure nothing has been disturbed. As I look over the desk once more and check my pockets to see that I've got the tools that I came with and my notepad, my hand closes on a book of matches, the sort of thing I routinely pick up. But these are from the café in Jackson Hole. On impulse, I drop them on the floor by the corner of the desk.

Before cracking the front door and looking out, I listen for sounds of anyone in the corridor. No one seems to be around. I lock the door before closing it and head toward the elevator.

There is a pay phone on the corner of the park near the beach, only a few blocks from here. I drive there, park the Buick beneath some Australian pine trees, and sit for a moment dreaming up something to say. Finally, I walk to the phone and dial Page Anderson. She picks up on the second ring, a hint of curiosity in her voice.

"Is Roy there?" I ask.

There is a brief hesitation. "Who's calling?"

"Don." I repeat Page's phone number, telling her that Roy had given it to me.

"Oh. Well, he isn't here."

"Do you expect him?"

"Actually, he's out of town. I don't expect him before next week, no." Something in her voice makes me think that she is happy that Roy has given someone her number.

"Sorry to bother you, Mrs. Emerson."

Page laughs. "We're not actually married."

"Oh, I seem to remember Roy telling me he was getting married. I assumed—"

"In June."

"What?"

"We're getting married in June."

"I guess that was it. Well, congratulations."

"Thanks. I'll be happy to take a message and have him call you."

"I'm just passing through and thought I would call. I'm going to be traveling for a while and unreachable."

"And your name again."

"Yes, of course. Don. He'll know who it is."

"Well, I'll certainly tell him you called. Is there any message?"

"Oh, no. We knew each other out West. He'll know what it's about."

"All right."

"Nice talking to you. And congratulations again."

I hang up.

The sulfuric stench of rotting seaweed drifts across the road from the beach. An odor that carries the toxic quality of gas that has suddenly been released from its stoppered container, the kind of smell that would send a chemistry class full of kids into fitful laughter. The unmistakable reek of something dead and decomposing. All from a weed aimlessly adrift on the surface of the sea, tugged and pulled by the wind, by currents and the tide, some of it eventually piling up onto a shoreline, and the beauty and the mystery is that it should pile up here, spreading its noxious aroma along a beach that is crowded with the condos and private homes of the rich.

Beautifully mysterious, and ironic. How a guy like Roy Faulkner Emerson should have to live surrounded by a stench that fits him to a T.

41

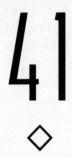

◇

Roy shows up the next morning at five minutes before ten. He is wearing jeans, a crisp white shirt, a pair of soft leather moccasins on his feet. His face is freshly shaved, and in the breeze stirred by the overhead fan, I get a whiff of the lingering scent of cloves. The crooked smile creases the lines around his mouth together, but there is something more in his face now. A certain tension that I have not seen in him before.

"Well, Bud, you ready to go for a ride?"

"I'm not much of a traveling man."

"Oh? That's not what I hear." Roy smirks. And for a second I think he has heard about my trip to Jackson Hole. It is conceivable that he still has contacts there. If so, then he may well have put two and two together and come up with an answer to the mysterious intruder in his condo last night. I am relieved when he says, "Gaby tells me you've been away on a trip."

"Work," I reply. As if that one word can dull whatever pleasure some people might get from travel.

"So how about it? I know a good seafood place up the Keys. We leave now, we can have lunch there and I'll get you back by two o'clock."

I shrug. "Work," I repeat. "I don't have time."

For a moment I am surprised when Roy appears to be sincerely disappointed. Hurt. "Anything interesting?"

"I don't discuss my cases."

"Just curious. I've often wondered how you guys do what you do."

"Why? You looking for another career?"

Roy grins. "As long as we're not going anyplace, mind if I sit?"

I motion to the chair in front of my desk and Roy sits down. I take a seat behind the desk. "This is the way it begins, right? A client comes in, sits down, and tells you his problem. You ask a few questions, then go out and solve the problem."

"Something like that."

"That must make you feel pretty good. Solving people's problems."

"Sometimes."

"I mean, for example. Let's say I got somebody bugging me. I want to find out who it is, what they want, and get them off my back. Now, in theory, I come to you, and you take care of it for me."

"In theory."

"And to do that you might have to snoop around some, am I right?"

I nod, feeling another twitch of discomfort.

"Would you break into somebody's house? I mean if I had hired you and you felt it was necessary to solve my problem?"

Clearing my throat, I say, "I'd rather not break the law."

"Of course. But in the interests of your client?"

"Sometimes there is a fine line, and sometimes you are forced to step over it." I concentrate on staring Roy in the eye.

Roy does not blink. Finally, he grins. "Isn't that just a poke in the eye with a sharp stick."

"What's that?"

"Legal beagles. Always ready to break the law to make the law."

"What are you getting at, Roy?"

"Somebody broke into my place last night."

"What's that got to do with me?"

"I think it was a shamus."

"Why would he want to break into your place?"

"Because somebody was paying him to snoop."

"I see." I feel my scalp begin to tingle. "That's what this is all about. Have you got something to hide?"

Roy looks slightly amused. "Everybody's got something to hide. Don't you?"

I think about it. All the past trials and tribulations with my difficult family, the marriages, the years of heavy drinking. Yeah, along the way there have been awkward and embarrassing episodes, things that I would just as soon let molder away in my own interior attic, but I have never killed anyone; nor have I committed bigamy. "Sure," I say to Roy, "but nothing I can't live with if it got out in the open."

"If it gets out in the open, that's one thing. If it's pried out that's another."

I force a smile. "What skeletons have you got hanging in your closet, Roy?"

Roy does not return the smile. "Papers. Business stuff. It gets into the wrong hands and I'm dead."

"So, what you're saying is that you're a victim of corporate espionage? Somebody's spying on you for business purposes. Is that it?"

"What I'm saying is that somebody broke in my place last night."

"They take anything?"

"I don't know yet."

"You call the police?"

Roy scoffs. "More legal beagles."

"So what do you want me to do?"

"Nothing. I'm just telling you, since you're in the same slimy line of work."

"What are you going to do?"

"Don't worry. I can handle it myself."

Two thoughts cross my mind, causing relief and concern at the same time. One, Roy does not suspect me. And two, I should call Don Cameron as soon as Roy leaves.

42

◇

Roy's face contorts once more, and that devil-may-care grin returns. I try to picture him on the mountain trail with Karen Hargreaves on the last day of her life and wonder what expression he wore just before she took the tumble.

Roy spreads his hands, looking up at the ceiling. "Amazing. A place like this, anywhere else in the world and you couldn't give it away. A shack."

"Location, location, location." I repeat Frank Pappagallo's mantra.

"Exactly." Roy leans forward. "But you're still asking too much. Now, let's talk turkey."

"Turkey?"

"Why I'm here. Let's get an agreement."

"I gave Fred Pacey my price. I think I made it clear. He didn't tell you?"

"He told me. Now, can we talk?"

"I hope I don't stutter. It's a take-it-or-leave-it kind of deal."

"Not in real estate; it doesn't work like that. There's always room for some negotiation."

"And arson."

"For the sake of our relationship I'll pretend I didn't hear that."

"You're pretending not to hear a lot of things, Roy. There's nothing to negotiate."

Roy picks up the leather satchel that is beside his chair. "You got a minute, I'd like to show you something."

"A minute's just about all I've got."

Roy pulls out some papers from the satchel and spreads them on the desk. "Here are the plans. I thought you might like to have a look at them."

I look over the sketches of the mall that's planned for here. Little blue lines in the shape of buildings with numbers, dimensions, some palm trees and a fountain drawn in. Except for the precision, they could be a child's drawings. "Okay. What am I supposed to say?"

"You know what these represent?"

"Buildings. Sure, I see them."

"Yeah, but the establishments themselves. The names are down there in fine print. Let me show you." Roy stands up and leans over the desk. Taking a pen from his shirt pocket, he points out some of what's to be built here. "We've got commitments from these outfits. They're on board. See that one? Bazoombas."

"Bazoombas?"

"Bazoombas. You know, the chain outfit. Bar, women in skimpy costumes." Roy makes a motion with his hands, holding them in front of his chest. "It's going in next door. The little grocery store that burned."

"Classy."

"You like it? Open till two or three in the morning. Tends to draw the young crowd. Spring-break types. Now, here's one. A store that's going to sell motorcycle paraphernalia, with a coffee bar and a café inside. It's been real popular in New York and on the West Coast. We look for it to draw a biker crowd, along with the wannabes, of course. And then there's the usual assortment of clothing stores and one upscale restaurant. All in all, we expect to have pretty much around-the-clock traffic through here. Like it?"

"Maybe it will be good for my business."

"Maybe. But somehow I don't think the people who come through here will be looking for shamuses."

"You never know. It sounds like the kind of place that could generate a high crime rate."

"Don't be a fool, Bud. You know as well as I do life is going to be pretty miserable if you're trying to live here."

"Life can be that way sometimes. You take the good with the bad."

"But not if you don't have to. We're offering a tidy sum so you only have to take the good."

"Yeah, but it isn't my sum."

"So we're back to that." Roy begins to fold up the drawings.

I nod. "We're back to that."

"You won't even think about five hundred thousand dollars?"

"I'll think about it. I'll think about it a lot. But you can come back here a hundred times with plans for an airport and a zoo, and I'll tell you the same thing. I told Fred Pacey—"

"Spare me, Bud. You don't need to keep repeating yourself."

"Apparently, I do. You're not getting the message."

Roy crams the papers in his satchel. "Don't be a fool, Bud."

"You're repeating yourself."

Roy's grin flickers, turning into a twitch before he walks out the door.

I'm left sitting alone thinking about $500,000. After the down payment on the family home on William Street, I'd still have a pretty nest egg. But I would have to live with the notion that I'd been robbed. And Pop had been burned out. Neither of those notions are acceptable.

It is ten-thirty, eight-thirty in Jackson Hole. I get myself a ginger ale and look up Don Cameron's office number.

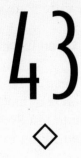

43

◇

Am I wrong about Roy? I wonder as I dial the Wyoming number. Am I simply pursuing another man's obsession? Anything's possible, I realize, but because of Gaby I cannot retreat.

Don's voice comes across the line, the slow western drawl like the sound of the wind along a dry river bed. I can picture him in his office, the Stetson pushed back on his head, the thick droopy mustache covering his mouth, and his booted feet propped up on the corner of the desk.

Without mentioning this morning's encounter with Roy, I bring him up to date on Roy's other involvements. When I am finished, Don whistles softly and says, "Well, that squares."

"You think he's feathering his nest?"

"What else? What do you know about Page Anderson?"

"Not a thing. That's next on the agenda."

"Ten will get you twenty she's got no problem with cash flow."

"The thought has crossed my mind. Maybe you can give me a hand."

"Sure. What do you need?"

I tell him about the book of matches from the café in Jackson Hole that I planted in Roy's apartment and the call to Page I made identifying myself as Don. No last name.

That bit of information doesn't seem to bother him. "So assuming she's told Roy, he thinks I'm in Florida tailing him."

"That's exactly what he thinks. Does he know you?"

"We never had the pleasure. But he certainly knows *of* me."

"And why you would be tailing him?"

"Of course."

"And maybe a little surprised that after all these years you have tracked him down again."

"I would think so."

"Good. Why not give Anderson an anonymous call from your office. Bring her up to date on Roy's marital status."

"Why anonymous?"

"I've already talked to her, so she probably would pick up on the difference in our voices."

"Why don't you call her then?"

"For one thing, she's got caller ID. Maybe that doesn't reach across state lines, but even if it does, a call from your office will add some weight to it. For another, I'd rather have Roy believing you were in Jackson Hole."

"Kind of a scattershot tactic, isn't it, Gideon?"

"Kind of."

"Doesn't it put the two women in some jeopardy?"

"I've thought about that," I tell him. "In fact, give it a day before you make the call. And give her Gabriella's phone number."

"Sure."

After giving him Gaby's number, I ask about the Hargreaves.

"Getting older," Don says. "Just like the rest of us."

"Well, pay my respects."

"I'll do that. And take it easy. Sounds like you're close to having a tiger by the tail. Be careful you don't get bit."

"I'll do that, Don." Then I hang up.

Don, of course, is right. I am putting Gaby at risk. And possibly Page Anderson. It isn't going to be easy, but I know I have to tell Gaby, have to convince her that the man she is married to, besides being a two-timer, may also be a murderer about ready to strike again. And I need to enlist her help in catching him.

After digging out the Miami phone book, I look up Hoke Moseley, a retired cop I know who has gone into private practice.

"What's doing?" I ask, when he answers the phone.

"Just sitting around in a blue funk waiting on you to call, Gideon. How's by you?"

"I don't want to waste your time with my complaints."

Hoke laughs. "Time, I've got."

"I'd rather take it up getting a little job done."

"How little?"

"I need some background information on someone in your area. A short bio will do."

"Does someone have a name?"

"Page Anderson. She lives in Coral Gables." I give him the address and telephone number.

"You're making it too easy. I thought I was going to have to work. When do you need it? Yesterday?"

"That would have been nice. But today will do."

"Okay. So I do get to work. I'll be in touch."

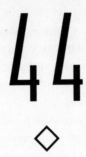

44

◇

The club is crowded with costumed revelers when I show up to play at nine o'clock. Ronnie greets me with a mile-wide grin, the kind that says the tip jar is overflowing. "Going to the parade tomorrow night?" she asks.

"How can I miss it? I've got a front-row seat."

Ronnie winks and hurries off to fill drink orders. The noise is a steady crescendo of voices and laughter as more and more people file into the dimly lit, smoke-filled room. I mount the stage to the piano and strike a couple of chords that quickly become lost in the bedlam.

Tomorrow night's parade down Duval Street is the culmination of several days of public partying, a time of mayhem and silliness, when strangers can let down their inhibitions for a night without any clear excuse other than the one of tradition, which fifteen years of celebrating Halloween in this fashion has produced. The town seems to be full, expectant. Upbeat. Next week the city will return to its senses as business groups begin to add up the revenue. And, at the same time various religious and conservative elements will continue to challenge the weeklong debauchery, urging the city to restrain the more flagrant and outrageous libertarians at next year's festival.

Tinseltown is this year's festival theme. I recognize a few attempts at creating Hollywood characters, but for the most part the costumes are generic, feathers and masks. And a lot of body paint.

A few people gather around the piano, clapping and singing, as I pound out a chorus of "When the Saints Go Marching In." Always a crowd pleaser. The circle around the piano grows. "I want to be in that number," someone croons in counterpoint.

"Wait your turn," another voice shouts, drawing a laugh. Everyone begins to clap.

I wind up with a vibrant two-handed trill that would have made Jerry Lee Lewis proud, and people begin to shout out requests. For an hour I play old standards, mostly show tunes that encourage a kind of rowdy sing-along as well as tips that begin to fill the oversize balloon brandy snifter that rests on the baby grand.

The crowd seems expansive, expectant. An easy gig. For an hour and a half I play nonstop before taking my first break. After a pit stop, I carry a glass of seltzer out on the balcony to brace myself with some fresh air.

The night hums, tight as a string on a bass fiddle. Pedestrians prowl Duval Street like fat in search of a sizzle. A car horn honks; someone shouts. Laughter erupts from the street, carried upward on the scented breeze—a mixture of exhaust fumes, sweat, and beer.

Back inside, the crowd has grown, fanned out. The mood has changed, and no amount of trickery will induce them back to the piano again. A woman wearing body paint and little else comes in with an entourage. Her small breasts, painted red, white, and blue in concentric circles have become like wheels, each nipple a hub to which a small flashing light has somehow been attached.

She is surrounded by guys in some sort of cavalry uniform, denim blue shirts with double button fronts, tight khaki trousers tucked into calf-high, lace-up boots. And Stetsons. They form a phalanx, escorting her to the bar, where Ronnie takes their drink orders. The cavalry looks on proudly, as if they are on a mission.

It is steadily downhill from then until my gig ends at two in the morning. Drinks are spilled. A fight breaks out between one of the cavalrymen and a civilian who stares too long at the painted lady. A bouncer comes and separates them before anyone is hurt, tossing the civilian out, while allowing the cavalryman to remain. A married couple dressed in space suits get into an argument at the bar.

By the end of the night the costumes seem to have wilted. The mood has gone as flat as a week-old open container of Coke. What was once excitement has now turned to rancor and irritation. I walk over to the bar, where Ronnie appears frazzled.

"Jesus!" she says. "Is it worth it?"

"Just a dress rehearsal for tomorrow."

She shakes her head. "No, this is the big night. Tomorrow they tank up early and are out of here by parade time. Except for the stragglers. When are you back here?"

"Next weekend."

"Lucky you. Take it easy, Gideon."

"You too, Ronnie."

Carrying a plastic cup of seltzer, I go out and walk

down Duval. People are still prowling, but the debris of
the night lies in the gutter, the trash cans full of dis-
carded beverage containers, a slightly sickening sour
smell hanging over the street. In a doorway a young guy
plays the saxophone, stumbling over some early Col-
trane, bobbing his horn when I toss a fiver into his open
instrument case.

At home there is a message on the machine from
Hoke Moseley. He has the information I requested, and
I can call him before eleven or after seven tomorrow
morning. This morning.

After a long cool shower, I hit the sack and fall into a
dreamless sleep.

45

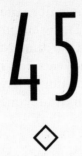

◇

It is bright and sunny the next morning, too bright and too sunny. I can still taste last night's residue of second-hand smoke and booze. Between that and less than five hours sleep, I feel as if I have crawled out of a Mexican cantina after a night of mariachi music and cheap tequila. Mouthwash doesn't help. The only hope is coffee, which I'm forbidden.

A few minutes before eight I sit down at my desk and phone Hoke in Miami.

"Brother, Gideon," he says, "age has its rewards. We don't need so much sleep."

"I need it. I just can't get it."

"Soon enough, my friend. Soon enough." Hoke laughs.

"You've got something for me on the Page Anderson woman?"

"I do. She's thirty-five years old, widowed once, and has no sign of financial problems. And did I mention? Easy on the eyes as well. Any help?"

"It fits a pattern. Where does the money come from?"

"She married well. Page started out in the entertainment business. Worked the dinner-theater circuit around south Florida for a few years, but her career never took off. When she was pushing thirty, she made the club scene as a singer. Under the name Page Paradise. Ever heard of her?"

"Nope."

"That was the problem. Which was where her husband entered. Bob Anderson. A big shot in the tire business. You've probably seen his ads on TV."

"I don't have a TV."

"Oh. Well, he did a song-and-dance routine. Kind of corny, but I guess it sells tires. Page even made a few ads with him."

"What happened to him?"

"Cancer. Leukemia. Took him in less than a year from the time he was diagnosed."

"How long ago?"

"About two years."

"And what's Page been doing in that time?"

"About a year ago she made an effort to revive her career, but she'd been away from it too long and there wasn't much to revive in the first place. Besides, with what she got from the tire mogul she doesn't need a career. She's got a house in the Gables, and when she needs money, all she's got to do is clip a coupon."

"Doesn't sound like much of a life."

"Which is maybe why she wants to get married again."

"The only problem with that is the fella she's picked out is already married."

Hoke remains silent for a moment. "So that's what this is about. I've been wondering."

"That's what it's about."

"Who are you working for?"

"A family out of state. This has happened before with not so pretty consequences."

"I see. Well, if there's anything more I can do, I'll just be sitting around on the porch watching the sun go down."

"Thanks, Hoke. What do I owe you?"

"A C-note will do."

"Done. I'll put a check in the mail today."

"And keep me posted."

"Sure thing."

After hanging up, I write a check out to Hoke, put it in an envelope, and drop it in the mailbox on the way to breakfast at the drugstore.

The information Hoke has provided is interesting but about what I had expected. At least I've got a take on Page Paradise Anderson, and something to think about. Like what she will do when she gets a call from Don Cameron this morning.

It is close to ten o'clock when I get back home and do what chores need doing around the house. At ten-thirty, just as I'm about ready to go out again, Frank Pappagallo shows up.

"Bud, for heaven's sake, why won't you listen to reason?"

Frank has on a straw hat, imitation Panama with a black band and the brim turned down all around. With his large nose and sallow complexion he looks ridiculous.

"I'm always willing to listen to reason. She just doesn't speak much anymore."

Frank sidles into the office. "Pacey's furious. He's threatening to withdraw his offer, to build around you."

I snicker. "I know. Surrounded by big bazoombas and Harleys. Life in the fast lane."

"Come on, Bud. I'm trying to do you a favor. What's a hundred grand?"

"I'll tell you what it is. It's a price tag. It means you can be bought. I won't be bought by a lowlife like Fred Pacey, no matter what I have to live with."

Frank lifts the hat by the brim and scratches his head with the same hand. Then puts the hat back on again. "What's it going to get you, Bud?"

"To sleep at night."

"All right." Frank sidles back to the door in the same herky-jerky way he came in. "Don't blame me if this blows up in your face."

I don't like the expression. "Cut the crap, Frank. If this blows up in my face, I'll hold Pacey, *and you,* responsible. You've known me too long for that. I won't be bought and I can't be pushed."

We stand eyeing each other, waiting. Finally, Frank sees there is no advantage to it and goes out the door in disgust.

I stay at my desk wondering if my pride has got the best of me. After half an hour of that, I say to hell with it, get the keys to the Buick, and leave the house.

46

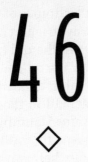

On my way out of Key West I think about stopping at Gaby's. Sooner or later she is going to hear something. From Page, or Roy. Or both of them. And she is going to blame me. By not stopping I am postponing the inevitable, but I will see her tonight for sure at the private party she is giving at the Blue Moon. The inevitable can wait a few hours.

Instead, I drive. With nowhere to go and no reason to get there, I head up the Keys, thinking of Roy, who so much likes to do business out of his car while on the road. Usually, I detest this sort of aimless driving but it does have certain benefits. Drifting and dreaming. The radio on, the music turned low; a warm, deliciously dry breeze floating in on a late October morning. A perfect time for reflection.

The traffic coming into Key West is a steady crawl of cars, vans, and buses. Judging from the expressions that I am able to catch a glimpse of now and then, it is a rowdy crowd on the way to a party.

Along the walkways of the old bridges, a few fishermen stand, leaning over the rails waiting for something to bite. The water is calm, about the color of a green tomato just on the vine. Off in the distance I can see a few flat's boats, the guides standing like scarecrows on their platforms built over the outboard engines, from whence they slowly pole their way across the shallows. Some commercial boats are out, too, working their traplines. The unholy alliance of industry and tourism, all right here along the highway, competing for a buck.

Coming into one of the many indistinguishable hamlets that dot the roadside through the Keys, I pass a service station and a convenience store before turning into and parking the Buick in the dusty lot of a shack that bills itself The Long Spoon Café.

Two wooden booths and half a dozen rickety tables are empty inside the screened-in porch. I perch on one of the counter stools and order iced tea from a waitress with stringy gray hair and an expressionless face that is wrinkled as a dried prune.

"Anything else?" she asks, putting the glass of tea, some of which slops onto the counter, in front of me.

"How's the fish sandwich?"

"Fresh."

"The only way I like it. Any particular fish or just whatever happens to be biting?"

"Today it's snapper, and don't ask what kind of snapper, because I don't know."

"I wouldn't dream of it. I'll take one."

"Fried or grilled?"

"Next you're going to offer me the wine list." That gets nothing from her. "Fried," I say.

The waitress makes a couple of ticks on her bill, tears it from the pad, and slides it under a bell in a hole in the wall that connects to the kitchen. Then comes back and puts down a napkin, anchoring it with a knife and fork.

"Kind of quiet for this time of day, isn't it?" I ask, continuing my quest for conversation.

She eyes me through narrow, dark slits. "What time of day is it?"

I look at my watch. "Lunchtime."

"Early," she says, swiping at the spilled liquid with a rag that looks like it has been used to clean oil sticks.

I just shrug rather than press the issue. The waitress moves away. I hear the sizzle of my fresh fish as it hits the fat in the kitchen. Five minutes later the waitress puts a platter in front of me with the fish on Cuban bread and some potato chips.

"You ain't a tourist, are you?" she asks. The eyes have opened a crack.

"Nope. Born and raised about twenty-five miles down the road from here."

"I thought so. Your accent." I sense that I have somehow paid my dues into this club. And wonder, like Groucho Marx, if I really want to be a member here.

"Key West?" she asks.

"Yeah. Maybe here you consider anyone down there a tourist, though."

"I lived in Key Weird a few years. It was all right. Until it got to be overrun."

"Don't let the chamber of commerce hear you. They regard that kind of talk as subversive."

"Screw the chamber of commerce. Tourists stop and take a look in here, they usually turn around and go straight back to their cars."

I let that pass, since I have no difficulty believing her. "How's the sandwich?"

"Any fresher and I'd have to thump it with a stick."

A smile almost adds another crease to the crone's face. Instead, she turns to the coffee urn, empties out the sludge, and rinses the pot before making a fresh batch. Then she disappears.

I finish my sandwich as a couple of fishermen come in, their T-shirts stained with dried blood and what looks like fish entrails. The waitress comes out of nowhere and, without speaking, draws two drafts into chilled mugs, putting them in front of the two men. Then walks over to me.

"Anything else."

I lift out my wallet and put a ten-dollar bill on the counter. "How'd they come up with the name for this place?"

The waitress snaps the ten between her fingers, carries it over to the register, rings up the sale, and brings back my change. "Check out the sign next to the door on your way out."

Leaving a couple bucks on the counter, I pocket the rest of the change and walk to the door. The sign next to it is old, scarred, and stained. "If you dine with the devil," it reads, "bring a long spoon."

◇

Surprisingly, there are no messages on the answering machine when I return home late in the afternoon. I have been expecting to hear something from Gaby, or at least Don Cameron, but silence is loudest perhaps just before the clamor.

Sitting down at the desk, I put in a call to Don. He does not answer, neither at the office nor his home. Putting my feet up on the desk, I stare out the window.

Duval Street has been closed off, and a glut of pedestrians in costumes fill the street, a kind of warm-up act to the grand parade that is scheduled to start in less than two hours.

From a dime store I have purchased a black half-mask, the kind made famous by the Lone Ranger so many decades ago. It will do little to conceal my identity, but it does fulfill the requirement in Gaby's invitation.

Half an hour before the parade is to begin, I shower and shave and put on a clean pair of khakis with a freshly laundered white shirt. Then, as I stand before the bathroom mirror feeling somewhat foolish, I pull on the black mask, surprised by the change it renders. I, at least, barely recognize the portly gentleman who stands half-masked before me.

It is dark when I go out to join the throng. Multitudes have crowded in on this narrow piece of asphalt—estimates from those who keep tabs on such things are that more than fifty thousand people will be on Duval tonight, a street that is less than a mile long. That seems like a staggering number, since it represents almost twice the normal population of this island.

Walking in the street toward the Blue Moon, I am quickly lost among the fray. The mostly elderly, early-bird observers craving front-row seats have brought their folding lawn chairs and are seated curbside, sipping drinks from their portable coolers, talking with their neighbors, and watching the spectacle with what appears to be an uncertain mixture of bemusement and outrage.

A guy in a Richard Nixon mask and a long raincoat prowls the edge of the street, waving one hand over his head in the familiar Nixon cliché before suddenly opening his raincoat to reveal a rubber phallus hanging down below his knees.

Various Disney creations scamper by: the mouse and the duck and the three little pigs. Little Red Riding Hood is pursued by the Big Bad Wolf, who is also in a raincoat, which he pops open on occasion to reveal equipment similar to Nixon's. Guys on stilts and bare-breasted women in body paint wiggle and dance. Cowboys and Indians and an array of movie characters dance by to shouts from the crowd. Tinseltown has come to Key West.

By the time I reach the Blue Moon, I am sweating. Beyond the lighted glass windows of the restaurant, the invitation-only crowd has gathered inside, all in considerably more elaborate costumes than the one I am wearing. Opening the door, I step into the dizzying, heady aroma of the party.

"Bud, I would have recognized you anywhere."

There is something familiar in the exaggerated, southern-accented voice, but at first I don't recognize it. It is not Gaby's. The woman is dressed in Victorian gown and a wig with long curly ringlets and a mask, and I assume she is meant to be Scarlett O'Hara. Clark Gable as Rhett Butler stands beside her.

"All I can say is, I don't give a damn," I say.

There are squeals of laughter from Scarlett, and a polite smile from Rhett as I make my way to the bar, where Humphrey Bogart in a white dinner jacket is dispensing drinks.

"What'll it be, Bud?" Bogart asks in a stagey voice, around the edge of a cigarette.

"Shirley Temple," I say, having no idea who the guy is behind the mask.

"She's around somewhere." Bogart laughs. He mixes my drink, hands it to me, then drawls, "Play it again, Sam."

Next to the bar a woman in a tuxedo, her short hair slicked back, begins singing "Strangers in the Night," doing not a bad imitation of Frank Sinatra.

Gaby has cleared out the tables and a few couples dance on the waxed hardwood floors. In one corner a buffet has been set up with some trays of hors d'oeuvres, kept filled by the kitchen staff, whose faces have been painted in black and white with elf caps covering their heads.

Among the revelers, I look for someone I recognize, but finding no one, carry my drink to a corner near the window where I can stand and keep an eye both on the street and the proceedings inside.

"What do you think, Bud? You like it?"

The voice is Frank Pappagallo's. The costume is Carmen Miranda. My lawyer is in blackface and drag, a basket of fruit perched precariously on his head. I stare at him with incredulity.

"It was my wife's idea," Frank says, a little apologetically it seems.

"Nice, Frank. You going to eat the fruit when you get home?"

Frank laughs, the bodice of his south-of-the-border-style dress jiggling with the water-filled balloons that provide his cleavage. " 'Eat the fruit.' That's rich, Bud. Maybe before the night's over. Great party, isn't it?"

"Beautiful."

Frank wanders away. I peer out the window. The cavalry, or whatever they are meant to be, some of whom were in the club last night, are marching by and tossing beads to the crowd. Many of them are older guys, rather stout, red-faced, sweating profusely in their uniforms. I watch them, wondering where they have come from, and do a double take just as they pass out of my line of sight. One of them looks a lot like Don Cameron.

"Like to dance, Bud?" Scarlett O'Hara taps my shoulder.

The female version of Sinatra is belting out "You'd Be So Nice to Come Home To" as I follow Scarlett onto the floor. We do a little two-step shuffle, and there is something familiar in the feel of her body, the way she moves to my touch.

"You really didn't recognize me, did you, Bud?"

She has dropped the phony southern accent, and now I hear the voice of my first wife, Peggy Baker Lowry Maloney.

"Jesus, Peg," I say. "You're the last person I expected to see here, and in that getup."

Peggy smiles. "Jake and I don't get out much. We thought it would be a hoot."

Jake Maloney is Peggy's current husband. "Rhett?" I ask.

"Isn't he good-looking?"

"Better than Gable himself," I say, feeling Peggy swell with pride.

"Everything all right with you?" Peggy asks as the song ends.

"Just fine," I say.

Peggy smiles and toddles off to join her husband, whom I can see watching us from the bar.

"Bud, could I see you a minute?"

It is Gaby. She is wearing the hat and white veil with the fine mesh that hides her features, the one she wears to tend her bees. Her voice has a peremptory quality, and I realize I am being summoned like a lamb to the slaughter as I follow her across the crowded room to her tiny office off the kitchen.

48

◇

Gaby's office is cramped, with barely enough room for the two of us to stand. There is a small desk, its surface covered with restaurant trade magazines, receipts and order forms, and business ledgers. Some filing cabinets take up the remainder of the floor space. All the intricacies of running a successful restaurant tucked in a cubbyhole. Gaby stands behind the desk, leaving the white veil, which resembles chain mail, to shroud her face. This is going to be difficult, perhaps easier done behind masks, I think.

"Just one question," Gaby says. "Why?"

From beyond the door, the sounds of laughter, kitchen staff, and the "voice" of Frank Sinatra blend and quaver.

"I was trying to protect you."

"Protect me?" Gaby's voice breaks slightly. "Do I look like a woman who needs protection, Bud? After all the years you've known me. Please. I'm not some waif, dependent on men, who breaks into tears whenever I've been hurt. I thought you knew me better than that, Bud."

"I do. You aren't that kind of woman. But what you are is in love. Maybe that's blinded you."

Gaby slowly shakes her head. "I don't think that's for you to decide, Bud."

"I was in the middle of an investigation. I still am. Looking for evidence, some proof of a crime."

"And did you get it?"

"Nothing that I could bring to you that would have changed your mind. I tried making certain suggestions, remember? You accused me of being jealous."

"Well, aren't you?"

"Not at this point."

Gaby shifts uneasily on her feet. "Who is this woman in Miami?"

"Page Anderson?"

"Yes. She called me. It wasn't pretty. Did you put her up to it?"

"No. I stumbled across her by accident."

"She's coming down here, looking for Roy, she says."

"Where is Roy?"

"No idea. I haven't seen him since last night."

"Does he know about this?"

"You mean what I now know?"

I nod.

"He should. I called and left a message asking for an explanation. I haven't heard from him."

The air in the room is close. There are food smells, and the slightly musty odor of paper. Still, I can smell Gaby's scent, the subtle and familiar cologne that she wears.

"It may be worse than another woman."

"What are you talking about?"

"Roy may also be a murderer."

There is a visible shift in her center of gravity. Gaby's shoulders slump, her head tilts forward. She rests her fists on top of her desk as if to support herself. When she speaks, her voice is distant. "Bud, why don't you just tell me everything."

I do. Telling her about my trip to Jackson Hole, and the Hargreaves family. While describing the cloud of suspicion Roy is under out there, "Sinatra" is belting out an upbeat version of "Fly Me to the Moon." When I finish, Gaby slumps down in the straight-back chair behind the desk. She picks up a letter opener, twisting it in her hands.

"Bud, this is unforgivable."

"I'm sorry, Gaby. I didn't know any of this until I went out there. I didn't know you were going to get married as quickly as you did."

"No, you still don't seem to get it. We're not kids, Bud. We've got past lives. All of us. And you of all people, I would think, should understand that. When we were in the Bahamas, Roy told me about his life in Wyoming. What's unforgivable is that you would take it upon yourself to meddle to the extent that you have."

Gaby lifts the veil from her face, folding it back over the top of her pith helmet, which she pushes back on her head. An angry welt appears where the band of the helmet rested against her forehead. Her face is flushed, her eyes like dead coals.

"I'd like to talk to Roy."

Gaby shrugs. "I don't think that would be advisable."

"Do you know where he is?"

"No, I don't. I think you should go now, Bud."

Gaby stares at me, the look is clearly accusatory.

"I don't think you should go home tonight," I tell her.

Gaby continues to stare at me. "Stop being my daddy, Bud. It doesn't suit you."

"Gaby—"

"Leave me. Please. I want some time alone."

I hesitate. Gaby puts the letter opener down.

Opening the door, I step outside and get the force of the party in full swing. "Sinatra" is singing "Black Magic." Much of the crowd is gathered in front of the windows, and the parade has started. I head over to the nearly empty bar and order a club soda. Bogart has disappeared, and one of the jokers from the kitchen staff has replaced him behind the bar.

"Gaby knows how to throw a party, doesn't she, Bud?"

Frank has come up beside me. One of the water-filled balloons has burst, and the front of his dress is damp. The fruit arrangement on top of his head has begun to work itself loose, and one banana hangs like a yellow horn just above his left ear, while a bunch of red grapes spills over his forehead like curls of hair.

"You need to go to the ladies' room and freshen up," I tell him.

Frank smiles, trying unsuccessfully to prop the grapes up.

"Have you seen Roy?"

"No, I've been looking for him, though. I was expecting to see him here."

"Maybe he doesn't recognize you in drag."

"Cut it out, Bud."

"Sorry, Frank." I finish my water and see Gaby come out of her office and head into the kitchen, her head covered again by the veil. "I'll see you later," I say to Frank. "Keep your bazoombas up."

49

◇

aking my way back to the kitchen, I look for Gaby, who is nowhere in sight. When I stop one of the costumed staff to ask if she has seen Gaby, she says, "I think she just went out the back." Then scurries away carrying a plate of prosciutto wrapped around wedges of melon.

The back door gives off on a sidewalk leading to a parking lot. The smell of sweat and beer braces the humid, deathly still air. Walking back to the parking lot, I find Gaby's empty car. No one is around, so I walk back to Duval Street, where a Budweiser truck has stalled in front of the Blue Moon, the float it is pulling filled with half-naked women, their flesh a milky sheen under the klieg lights mounted on balconies along the street. The women's hands are raised in a fixed wave, like those of royalty, their red lips curled in ghoulishly frozen smiles. From loudspeakers on the float comes a

tinny-sounding rock tune, the jarring lyrics impossible
to make out in the pandemonium of the crowd.

I try to work my way up the street, but it is like swimming against an opposing current, impossible to measure much in the way of progress.

The club is only a block away, and what would normally be a three-minute walk takes me more than ten
minutes as I fight through the dense, roiling mob. After
taking the elevator up, I hurry over to where Ronnie is
tending bar, a few castaways having their plastic go-
cups filled.

"Have you seen Gaby?"

Ronnie looks at me blankly.

"From the Blue Moon."

"Oh, her. No, I haven't."

"She might have been wearing a funny hat with a
veil covering her face."

Ronnie's face brightens. "Yeah, just a few minutes
ago. I served her a drink and she went out. You must
have just crossed on the elevators."

"Was she alone?"

Ronnie nods.

I walk out onto the balcony overlooking the street.
There is a crowd here, too, although, despite providing
a bird's-eye view of the street, it does not seem like the
best vantage point from which to watch a parade.

For two or three blocks in both directions, I scan the
crowd, looking for Gaby. Amidst such a mob there seems
little chance of spotting one individual.

Because of their numbers and blue uniforms, a few
members of the cavalry outfit stand out in the crowd,
reminding me that earlier I thought I saw Don Cameron
among them. Which came as a complete surprise. What
would he be doing here, I wonder?

From the window of the Blue Moon the only fleeting glimpse I had was of someone about Cameron's build wearing a Stetson similar to the one Don always wore and with the same droopy mustache. On the other hand, most of these guys are wearing similar hats, and many of them probably have mustaches. And if it was Cameron, why had he not told me he was coming here?

If Cameron has flown all this way, then he is here, I am sure, on his own agenda that has to do with Roy, and not to march in a parade. The possibility that Don, in his quietly eccentric manner, is some kind of avenging angel does not escape me.

The parade stutters along, the music of several bands bouncing into the night air. Many of the floats are little more than commercial boosterism, a few ragged palm fronds stacked across a truck bed, some coconuts and bunting, advertising a local bar. A few of the floats, however, are elaborate.

A giant gorilla, affixed atop a scaled version of Key West's lighthouse, holds a screaming, partially clad woman, the gorilla's red eyes oscillating in their sockets. A tropical version of King Kong.

On the side streets beyond Duval it is dark, without traffic, as if the rest of the town has been abandoned for a few hours. And for half an hour I stand there transfixed as the parade moves along in its herky-jerky fashion, like a filmstrip being slowly pulled by hand through a lighted projector.

Finally, reluctantly, I ride the elevator down and rejoin the fray, plunging back into the crowd to look for Gaby. It is quickly apparent that it is unreasonable to think that I will find her this way.

By the time I have pushed and clawed my way

through the sweating throng, had drinks spilled on me, been cursed and spat on, the parade has reached its end, an intolerable cacophony of sound erupting as the mob begins to overrun the street.

I find myself pressed against one of the stray blue shirts, who is drunk, holding on to the waist of a young lady in a black cat suit. I ask him if he knows Don Cameron.

"Who?" The black cat puts both her arms around the soldier, and purrs.

"Don Cameron."

"Never heard of him."

"Would you know everyone in this outfit?"

"Hell, no. We come from all over the country. I don't know most of them."

He grins, takes a swig of his drink, and stumbles off with his feline friend.

It is useless to fight the crowd. I go along with its surge and flow, swept uptown in the direction from which I have come, sure that none of the downtown bars would attract Gaby. A few minutes later I come on another of the blue shirts and ask him about Cameron.

"Sure, he's around."

"Don Cameron from Jackson Hole?"

"Yeah, that's the one."

"Do you know where I can find him?"

"Nope. He was with us until a few blocks back, where I saw him drop out. He met up with a woman, I think."

What woman, I wonder? It doesn't sound like Don. Someone he knew? Somehow, I manage to dislodge myself from the crowd and cut over to a side street where King Kong on his lighthouse stands silenced, the eyes deadened, dark orbs. There is no sign of the screaming woman he had clutched in his fist.

Finally, I return to the Blue Moon, where the party goes on. When I ask around about Gaby, no one has seen her. Frank is no longer in the crowd, either. Scarlett O'Hara, aka Peggy Maloney, my ex-wife is standing at the bar with her husband Rhett Butler, aka Jake Maloney. I push my way through the tangle of bodies toward them.

"Peggy."

"Oh, hi, Bud. Did you see the parade? Wasn't it the best?"

So typically Peggy, childlike in her enthusiasm. I agree that it was spectacular. "Have you seen Gaby?"

Peggy looks at Jake. "Didn't we see her a while ago?"

Jake shrugs. "I think she was with Bogie," Peggy says, turning back to me.

"Bogie?"

"You know, the bartender."

Yes, of course. That Bogie. "How long ago?"

"Oh, Bud, I don't remember. Maybe half an hour ago. Why? Is something wrong?"

Her question falls on my retreating back as I turn away and head for the kitchen. The staff are congregated back there, beginning the clean-up process. Still in their black-and-white harlequin paint, a couple of them look up when I come in. "The bartender," I say. "Does anyone know who he was?"

Everyone looks around, shaking their heads. Someone points to a woman who is just coming in carrying an empty serving tray. I ask her. She says she thinks he was a stand-in. The regular bartender had called in sick at the last minute.

"But you don't know who the replacement was?"

No, she says, she has no idea. Gaby would probably know, but she has gone.

And I am left with the inescapable fear that Gaby is in danger. Whatever doubt may have crossed my mind earlier has been erased. I am willing to bet that behind the Bogie costume lurks a killer. Roy Emerson.

50

◇

Gaby's car is still in the parking lot behind the Blue Moon, its doors locked. Looking around the small lot, which is restricted during the day to area business parking only, I can see no sign of Roy's car. There is no reason why he would have parked here, but the fact that Gaby's car is here, his isn't, and Gaby was last seen leaving with the masked bartender leaves me with an uneasy feeling.

The crowd noise is spreading from Duval to the side streets as the party begins to break up. Foot traffic is beginning to disperse, and the sound of cars zooming off into the night fills the air, along with the squeal and roar from thousands of people trying to keep the party alive. A certain helplessness overcomes me when I realize that I have no idea where to begin to look for Gaby. If she has gone off with Roy, I don't even know if it was voluntary.

I can wait here at her car, but if she doesn't show up,

I'm wasting valuable time. The only sensible thing I can think to do is to go home and get the Buick and drive up the Keys to see if she's there. After another five minutes of hanging around and turning the limited options over in my mind, I set off for home.

It is after midnight, and as I approach my place, I am surprised to see Pop on the sidewalk in front of the shell of the old *groceria*.

"What are you doing down here, Pop?"

"We watched the parade." He seems to get older and smaller each time I see him; his dark eyes still have that haunted look.

"Where's the family?" I ask. There's still a mix of costumed people wandering up and down the street, some of them drinking from beer cans loosely concealed in small paper bags.

"They went home. I wasn't ready to go yet."

"It still hurts, doesn't it, Pop?"

He nods. The lights from the used-car lot across the street spill over us, but the dark gap where Pop's place used to be is a shadowy frame with a few burnt timbers still poking up from the ground, like dead tree limbs that have been scarred by lightning.

"I need to ask you something that's been in my mind for a while now, Pop." I stare into his eyes while he looks off into the distance.

"Sure, Bud."

"Do you blame me?"

He remains motionless, seeming to stare at something that is beyond my vision. I feel a cool trickle of sweat run down the base of my spine. Finally, Pop shrugs his shoulders. "Nobody to blame, Bud."

Something in his voice is off, though.

"Sooner or later they get you. There's no place for the little guy in this country."

Though his voice contains a quality of sadness, I know Pop is simply stating a fact, something he believes, and not feeling sorry for himself.

"It's a struggle, Pop. Always has been, always will be."

Pop nods. *"La lucha."*

"What's that?"

"Same thing. The struggle. So what you going to do, Bud?"

"Sell. If I can get my price."

"Be careful, Bud."

"Yeah, I will."

I offer Pop my hand. We shake, and I can feel his thin bony fingers, the flesh smooth as a washed stone in a creek. "And don't worry, Pop," I say. "This is for both of us."

Pop looks at me questioningly, and I feel his eyes on me as I turn and go into the house.

Sitting down at my desk, I pick up the phone and dial Gaby's number. No answer. After looking up Roy's number, I dial it. Again, nothing. I sit back and contemplate driving up to Gaby's. I am still sitting ten minutes later when I hear footsteps on the porch and someone knocks on the door.

It is nearly one o'clock. I walk over to the door and look through the slats in the blind. Don Cameron stands on the porch, his blue twill shirt darkened with sweat stains.

"Surprise," he grumbles when I open the door.

"Not quite. I thought I saw you in the parade tonight."

"I figured you would avoid that. Too much tourism."

"If I hadn't been working, I probably would have. Kind of unlike you to come all this way just for a parade, isn't it?"

"Working too. Bob Hargreaves asked me to come. Man, it's hot here."

"Can't they find a tropical uniform for you guys? You look like you're dressed for a reenactment of Custer's last stand."

Don shrugs, standing under the overhead fan while he mops the sweat from his brow with a blue bandanna.

"So you told Bob Hargreaves about Roy, and he sent you down here?"

Don nods. "Just in case."

"Just in case I couldn't handle the situation."

"No, nothing like that." Don glances around the room. "For Bob, even for me, it's personal. You know that. I wanted to be here. Bob would have come himself if he was in better shape."

"You planning on confronting Roy?"

"I don't know. From what you described on the phone, I'd say he was going to make a move. It sounds like he's been cornered."

"Maybe."

"Where is he?"

"I wish I knew."

"And his wife?"

"I was with her earlier. I don't know where she is now, and she's still defending Roy."

"That's not a good sign."

"I was getting ready to drive up to her place."

"You want company?"

I shake my head. "I'd rather you stake out Roy's place

in town. Just in case he shows up there. Have you got a rental car?"

Don nods.

"You can follow me and I'll show you where he lives."

51

◇

Driving up the Keys, I try to think of something more I might have said to Gaby, some approach I could have taken that would have been more convincing. As it is, I now no longer know what kind of a reception to expect when I encounter her.

Traffic is light, and half an hour later I pull into Gaby's drive. It is well after two o'clock in the morning. The place is dark. My headlights don't pick out any vehicles parked in the carport below the house. I shut off the lights and the ignition and sit for a moment, in the darkness. There are no sounds coming from inside the house.

In fact, the surrounding silence is deafening. The nearest house to Gaby's is a quarter of a mile away. She is tucked back here in a wooded hammock several miles from the highway. Each crackle of a dry thatch palm leaf brushing against another, the scuttle of lizards through the thick underbrush, and the whine of a mosquito now and then as it cruises in my open window, resonate like thunder over the silence. Unless she is in bed, sleeping soundly, it seems certain that if Gaby is inside, she will have heard my car when I drove up.

There are no streetlights back here, and stars are strewn across the sky like confetti. I open the car door and step out, the gravel drive crunching under my weight, and close the door quietly. A gentle rhythmic sighing, almost like breathing or a rusty hinge creaking against its holding pin, causes me to pause and listen. It is a sound so faint that it is hardly noticeable. Because there is no wind, it seems unlikely that the sound could be caused by a door swinging on its hinges.

Cautiously, I climb the steps, wishing I were carrying a gun. The creaking remains constant. On the landing at the top of the stairs I can look in the screen door, but everything is in darkness, with only the ghostly dim shadows of the furnishings visible.

A mosquito lands on my neck, and I slap at it, a sound that seems as loud as a rifle shot in my ear.

"Gaby," I call, my voice barely above a whisper.

There is no answer. I try the screen door. It is unlatched. Stepping inside and moving slowly into the room, I listen as the rhythmic creaking grows louder.

Walking into the main room of the house, I get a whiff of Gaby's perfume and, standing stock-still in nearly total darkness, reach out, my fingers fumbling along the wall where the overhead light switch should be.

There is a sudden flutter, something churning the air next to my face, and I flick the light on to see a giant black moth, the size of a bat, settling on the wall near the cornice just below the ceiling.

No one is in the room. Everything is in place. One of the overhead paddle fans, running on slow speed, makes the rhythmic bump and whine that I have been hearing. "Gaby?" I walk through the house, turning on lights and calling her name, but there is no one here, and nothing to indicate that anything is amiss.

When I return to the living room and look up at the moth, it looks like a dark stain on the wall—silent, motionless. Disturbing. After turning out the lights, I return to my car and sit there, uncertain what to do next.

There is nothing to do except wait. It seems only reasonable to believe that sooner or later Gaby will come home. Even though there's been nothing reasonable about this entire evening. It would be easy enough just to drive back to town, I think, go home and go to bed, which is what I would like to do. And, if it was anyone besides Gaby, that's exactly what I would do. Maybe I am feeling a little guilt because of her. Maybe I have handled this badly. Whatever, I have a hunch that what remains of the night isn't going to find me in my bed. About that at least, I'm not wrong.

Since I don't want her to see my car, I start the Buick and head back over to the main road, where earlier I passed a small marina that had a parking area with a couple of cars that had been left there. I pull in and cut the motor. She will have to pass by here on her way home.

A couple of residential streets lead off the main road along canals with houses built on either side of their banks. A quiet, peaceful little suburban setting. I can't see any lights, and there is no traffic along the road, and except for the fuzzy night sounds, it is still. Scrunching down in the seat, I put my head back against the cushion and close my eyes.

The sound of a distant car motor stirs me, and when I sit up and look at the clock on the dash, I see that it is almost five o'clock. I've got a kink in my neck, and my eyes feel heavy with sleep. The car is coming fast from the direction of the highway, and seconds later when it zooms by me, I see that it is Gaby's car, and in the brief seconds it takes to pass me, I think I see her reflection in the dash lights, but it is too dark to tell if there is anyone else in the car with her.

I wait, listening as the car slows down, and am about to start the Buick when another car goes by at a high rate of speed. Roy's car. I let another couple of minutes go by, then drive down to the turnoff to Gaby's and park along the road before setting out on foot on the less than a quarter of a mile to Gaby's.

When I get within sight of the house, I see both cars parked side by side outside the carport. A couple of lights are on in the house, one in the kitchen and another upstairs in one of the bedrooms. Standing near one of the parked cars, I can see only into the kitchen, beyond the front porch. I hear a toilet flush, and a pump comes on somewhere in the direction of the carport.

After a while Roy Emerson walks into the kitchen. He is wearing the white dinner jacket that he had on when he was tending bar in the Blue Moon. The Bogart mask is gone, and his black bow tie is unclipped, though still around his neck.

I watch as he opens the refrigerator and takes out a carton of eggs and begins breaking several of them into a glass bowl. Moments later the smell of bacon frying wafts across the sullen night air, followed by the scent of freshly brewed coffee.

Just then Gaby comes into the kitchen. She has changed clothes. She seems to be wearing a robe. She stands, leaning against the counter, watching Roy cook breakfast. There is something about her, something in her look that I can't put my finger on. Until she moves again. And says something I can't hear to Roy. He looks at her with dark, narrow eyes, his lip curled.

Gaby staggers slightly against the counter, then leans slowly into it. From the tilt of her head to the attempt at precision in each movement she makes, I recognize that she has had too much to drink.

52

◇

I continue to watch as Roy uncorks a bottle of white wine, pouring some into a glass, which he hands to Gaby. She stares at him. It is hard to read anything in her expression. She could be staring right through him, for all I know. I have no difficulty, however, reading the chilling smile on Roy's face as he walks up beside her, puts his arm around her shoulders, then picks up his own glass in his free hand and holds it toward her in a toast.

Gaby just stands there, leaning against the counter, staring at nothing. At least nothing that I can see. Then, slowly, she lifts the glass, seems to look at it for a moment before turning to Roy, and tosses the contents in his face.

Roy lifts his hand from her shoulder and wipes his face. He doesn't do anything about the grin. Gaby just stands there looking at him, and although her lips move, I can't hear what she says. Suddenly, Roy grabs her around the waist and pulls her against him, forcing his mouth over hers. Gaby shrinks back, her hands pressed against his shoulders, before slowly giving in to the kiss.

As they kiss, Roy runs one hand through her dark, tangled hair. Then he steps back, grinning down at her. Gaby holds on to his arms, weaving slightly. Roy pours more wine, and now Gaby clinks glasses with him.

As they drink, it begins to seem likely to me that this fight has been going on most of the night—what was left of the night, anyway, after Gaby left the Blue Moon this evening. I can imagine that they found an out-of-the-way bar where they sat and had a real scrap, the kind someone who has been put through what Gaby has been put through might provoke. All of the venom she'd stored up and would not release when I told her about Roy would have bubbled over once she was alone with him. In addition, there was the emotional toll she had suffered.

All of it fueled by alcohol, of course. And, Roy, I can picture, would have remained his usual cool, unshakable self, denying everything, always with a ready explanation. At closing time, still angry, Gaby would have insisted on coming home alone. Roy, the dutiful husband, would have followed.

If that is the way it happened, then what I have witnessed here is the culmination of that fight. They should be ready to go to bed and sleep it off, wake up later today to a clean slate.

Instead, I watch as Roy crooks a finger on the inside lapel of Gaby's robe, pulls the cloth open, and pours what's left of his wine down her front.

I can't see the expression in Gaby's eyes, but I do see her shudder. I wait for some other reaction from her, but it doesn't come. Instead, Roy pulls the robe open, exposing Gaby's breasts, and runs his hand across them. Then bends to take one of her nipples in his mouth. Gaby's head arches backward.

A gray dawn is beginning to push back the darkness, and I want to go home. There is something spiteful, even vindictive in the way Roy takes her, reaching for her under the folds of her robe, standing, Gaby's back pressed against the counter, her hands flung upward as if she is warding off blows until Roy collapses against her.

Later, Roy finishes cooking breakfast, and they sit now at the kitchen counter, eating. Gaby is still unsteady, eats little, nursing another glass of wine, while Roy packs it away as though it were his last meal.

By the time they have finished, there is enough light in the sky to make concealment impossible, and I am forced to move away, further back up the road and into some shrubbery that conceals not only me but also my view of Gaby and Roy.

I want to see the lights go out and the house to go quiet and know that they have gone to bed. Then I can linger around here for a while longer before walking back to my car and driving home to do the same. Tonight or tomorrow I can meet with Don Cameron and tell him I'm finished with Roy Emerson. If Bob Hargreaves wants any more service, he can get someone else to provide it. And I'll happily give him back his money, or some of it, to be done with this caper.

It has already cost me in nonnegotiable matters, and I'm no longer willing to pay further for someone else's obsession.

On the other hand, maybe I am just tired, bone tired,

and I'll think more clearly after several hours sleep and a decent meal. Maybe—but I don't think so.

In any case, I'm not given the opportunity. Fifteen minutes later, when I think everything has settled down, the screen door bangs and I see Roy, wearing a pair of swim trunks, come down the stairs, leading Gaby by the hand. She stumbles on one of the steps, and Roy keeps her from falling, then puts an arm around her waist as they walk down the dock toward the water.

I hear a splash, and moments later a shriek that could have come only from Gaby.

53

The first orange arc of the sun has penetrated the horizon as I run to the end of the dock. Shallow, even with the tide in, the surrounding water is luminous. Turtle grass shimmers like burnished silver just below the surface. A school of snapper hangs off the pilings, noses into the gently flowing current. For miles around it is soundless, a calm more suited to a pond than the fringe of the Gulf of Mexico.

A hundred yards out, at the edge of the channel, the pewter-colored water suddenly turns inky blue, demarcating deeper water. There I see Roy, his head bobbing like a cork. But no sign of Gaby.

"Roy!"

He turns toward my voice just as Gaby's face breaks the surface, one hand clutching at him, the other struggling to tread water, a tiny maelstrom in the midst of the calm.

Kicking off my shoes and stripping down to my boxer

shorts, I jump down from the dock and begin to swim toward them. Roy looks benign, a puppy caught chewing on his master's shoe. For a second he seems uncertain what to do, whether to flee or stay. Then, as I swim toward them, he cradles Gaby in the crook of his arm and begins sidestroking toward me.

I can hear Gaby sputtering, trying to cough up water.

"Current got her," Roy says, gasping for breath. "Help me get her back to the dock."

Once back in water shallow enough to stand in, we float Gaby between us, Roy holding her head out of the water, while her legs and arms dangle lifelessly from her naked body. She is alive, her skin cool—the cough less persistent now.

"Lucky you came along," Roy says as we get near the dock. "Don't know if I could have gotten her out of the water by myself."

Roy stands on the concrete supports and hoists himself up onto the dock while I hold Gaby. Then, as I lift her out of the water, Roy leans down and grabs her by the underarms, and together we heave and push her up onto the dock.

"You know any CPR?" Roy asks when I climb out of the water and bend down, pressing a finger against Gaby's throat to check her pulse.

"Yeah, but you'd better go call and get someone out here fast."

Roy hesitates. "By the way, what are you doing out here at this time of day?"

"Go on, man, if you want her to live."

We stare at one another for a second before Roy starts down the dock and I bend over and press my lips to Gaby's.

Her pulse is strong, and as I breathe into her, pushing

against her diaphragm, a trickle of water comes out her mouth. Her eyes open, flickering, as a spasm of coughing racks her body. She turns her head and vomits. Then lies flat, looking up at me. "Bud, is that you?"

"Yes," I say. "You're going to be okay."

"Where's Roy?"

"He's gone to get some help."

She shakes her head. "I don't want to see him." She tries to sit up, suddenly aware of her nakedness.

Picking up my shirt from the dock, I put it on her. Gaby coughs again, then sits holding her face in her hands as I pull on my khakis.

When she looks up, her eyes have cleared; there is a look of awareness on her face, as if she has just come home from a long journey, a look of recognition.

"What happened out there?" I ask.

Gaby pushes her hair back, then looks at me. "He tried to kill me."

I don't say anything.

"I'm sorry," Gaby says.

"You don't have anything to be sorry about."

"For blaming you."

"Forget it."

"I'm a fool, Bud."

"Just take it easy, Gaby."

"I tried to put my life on hold. I thought I was doing the right thing."

"Don't do this now." I sit down beside her and put my arm around her.

She stares out at the sea. "I've been so self-involved, determined to get everything in order."

"Gaby—"

"Let me finish, Bud. I couldn't see through Roy because I was in such a hurry. It was time. Time to get married. Time to raise a family."

I hear footsteps coming back down the dock.

"I thought I was doing the right thing, and when it was too late, I couldn't admit that I'd made a mistake."

"What mistake?" Roy asks.

Gaby and I both turn toward him. He is holding a gun, a little snub-nosed .38, not really pointing it at anyone, but that doesn't seem to provide any comfort.

"You, darling," Gaby says.

54

◇

It's all over, Roy," I say. "Your days as a Romeo are finished. Don Cameron flew in from Jackson Hole the other day. We know about Karen Hargreaves and the woman out in Idaho you drowned."

Standing there in his swim trunks, Roy, his eyes hooded, looks from me to Gaby, and back to me. The thin curl of his lip slips for a just a moment, then returns. "You like the sound of your own voice, dickus, or is this just some cheap theatrics?"

"Take your pick, Roy. Either way, the jig's up. The end of the road."

"We'll see about that." He raises the gun. "By the time the sharks get finished with you, there won't be enough of you left to put under a microscope."

"I wouldn't count on it. Looks like it's going to be a pretty day. Lots of boat traffic. Gunshots out here on the water will be heard for miles. Our bodies could be spotted and picked up before you get off the key."

Roy seems to consider that. "You've got a point. Let's go up to the house."

"Sure. You could kill us there, then torch the place. That's more your style, isn't it? Just like the grocery store you burned down in Key West."

"You're lucky I didn't get your shack."

"If Pacey didn't rein you in, you probably would have."

"Fred Pacey's a wimp. I controlled that project. He didn't have anything to do with it."

"He didn't approve the arson?"

"He thought it was his luck. Guys with money like that can afford to believe in luck. I've got to make my own. All of your detecting, you should know that."

"Just like in Jackson Hole? The trading post development you burned."

Roy grins now. "Okay, dickus, you've proved you're good at your job. Let's go and see how well you die."

Gaby and I stand up. She squeezes my hand as we start walking up the dock toward her house.

When we have walked beyond the mangrove shoreline into the wetland clearing leading to the house, Gaby stops. "Roy," she says, "don't do this. You can walk out of here. No one's got anything on you. I'm not going to press charges. Don't dig yourself in any deeper than you already are."

"Too late, Gabe. You should have thought of that when you hired Sam Spade here to dig into my past."

Gaby takes a couple of steps toward Roy.

"Stay back," Roy barks.

"Come on, Roy," I say. "You don't murder women in cold blood. You set up *accidents*. So there's never any hard evidence against you."

"I can make an exception."

JOHN LESLIE

"Gaby's right. Why start now?"

"Just turn around and keep walking."

"Roy, listen to me." Gaby takes a couple more steps in his direction, close enough now that she could reach out and touch him. But she just stands there.

"Forget it, Gabe."

Gaby looks back at me. I shrug.

On either side of the narrow dock are wetlands, hard caprock poking through the ground, and miniature wildflowers that look like weeds growing out of the caprock amidst the driftwood that sprouts like bleached bones. Nearby, Gaby's beehives are stacked two high on wooden bottom boards.

As Gaby turns toward me, she trips on a warped gray plank in the dock that has sprung loose from the piling, sticking up a couple of inches from the rest of the dock.

Roy instinctively bends toward her, lowering the gun as he does, a two-second distraction that allows me to hurl my body at him in a flying tackle, taking both of us down hard against the dock.

Roy manages to hang on to the gun, and I feel the butt of it hammer against my shoulder blade. Getting one knee planted on the dock, I throw my left hand up to grab Roy's wrist before he can hammer me again. I'm reaching for his neck with my right hand when he swings his knee up, clipping me good in the kidneys, then twists sideways as I try to hang on to his gun hand.

Working with twenty-five extra years and as many extra pounds, I realize I'm no match for Roy without getting the gun away from him.

I don't see Gaby, who has either jumped or been pushed off the dock in the tumult. Right now I don't see anything except the blue steel of Roy's snub-nosed .38. Sweat drips down my hairline.

I've still got a clamp on Roy's wrist, reaching up with my right hand to try to get another hold. Roy manages to struggle to his feet, pulling me against the rough plank boards as I feel my grip begin to loosen.

Suddenly, Roy jerks his gun hand free, and all I can do is grab a leg, upending him as the gun roars, the shot skying as Roy falls.

Lunging forward, I get my knee in his chest this time and both hands around his right arm, twisting it backward against the edge of the dock until Roy is forced to drop the gun, which clatters down against caprock.

I hear myself wheezing and gasping for air as I cock my fist and attempt to throw a punch into the side of Roy's face. He bucks and dodges; the punch lands a glancing blow off the side of his head as we both tumble over the side of the dock.

I feel the scrape of the hard Florida landscape against bare skin, prickly scrabble biting into my sweat-soaked body. Roy jumps to his feet and flings himself toward where the gun lies, while I struggle to my feet, propelled upward now only by adrenaline, seeing Roy poised over the .38, grasping it by the barrel, as I throw a punch, feeling my fist hit against his rib cage. Roy falls to the side against a piling. I rush him, pinioning his arms beneath mine, too tired now to do anything except hold on, like a boxer on the ropes.

We dance back, and as we do, I see Gaby floating in the distance, a kind of mirage, surrounded by a cloud of yellow and black, walking toward us, something hanging from her hand, enveloped in a scent of thick, flowery sweetness.

Roy seems to have seen her, too. He surges violently against me, ripping one arm free as Gaby begins to run and swing whatever it is she is carrying, swinging it back and forth, like it was something sacred, part of a ritual.

As Roy attempts to break free, I hang on, waiting until the cloud that surrounds Gaby swarms toward us. Bees. Thousands of them. Drifting over us like a toxic cloud. Settling on our bare skin, their welcome stings like pin pricks from a doctor's needle.

55

◇

At the house, Gaby picks up the phone and punches in some numbers. After a while she hangs up without speaking to anyone. I watch as she takes some ice from the freezer and brings it over to where I'm sitting, touching the ice to the red welts that have begun to swell where I've been stung. The cold is soothing.

From the deck we can see Roy on the ground where he fell, a few bees still hovering over his body.

"Charley, the doctor who came the last time, isn't home," Gaby says, rubbing the ice on my skin without looking at me. "I'm going to call 911 now, but it will take them a while to get here. There's nothing anyone can do for Roy. I should have had some epinephrine on hand, but I don't. Roy refused to get a prescription. 'Lightning doesn't strike the same place twice,' he told me." Gaby looks at me. "He was wrong, wasn't he?"

The look in Gaby's eyes is decisive, determined. "Sure, he was," I say.

"I'm going to get dressed, then go down to the dock and get the gun and toss it in the sea. Then, I'll put that hive back together and wait for the medics. When they get here, I'll be the grieving widow."

"Okay," I say. "But you may have to explain some of the bruises on Roy's body."

"He fell off the dock when he was stung."

"You don't have to do this, you know. It was self-defense."

"I have some pride, Bud. If you don't mind, I'd like to hang on to what's left of it." Gaby stands up. "The bees swarmed suddenly, unpredictably. We were in the wrong place at the wrong time."

"Sure."

"Just keep putting ice on those stings. Tomorrow they'll be itchy. You'll be okay. We both will."

I watch her from the back deck of the house as she goes about the tasks she designated. Twenty minutes later when the medics show up and put Roy's body on the stretcher, I go inside and make a phone call.

"Frank, Roy's dead. He was stung by bees."

"What happened?"

I relate Gaby's version. "I thought you ought to let Fred Pacey know."

"I'll do that," Frank replies.

"You might also want to tell him that Roy confessed to starting the fire at Pop's place."

"Bud—"

"Listen to me carefully, Frank. He said Fred doesn't know anything about it. And, I'm not going to make an issue of this unless I'm forced to. I want my price for the property and I want a hundred grand up front. Simple as that."

"I'll tell him, Bud."

The rest of the day Gaby tends to my wounds. There is no further mention of Roy. In the afternoon, I fall asleep on the couch for a couple of hours, and when I wake, it is to the smell of steak being grilled.

"Feeling any better?" Gaby asks when I join her in the kitchen.

"Hungry."

"I guessed you might be. I slept some, too, and woke up ravenous."

When we sit down at the table to eat, Gaby announces that she is going to take some time away from work. "I'm going to make some changes in the way I live."

"Good," I say.

"I've been thinking that I may need a chaperone."

I look at her. Her eyes are still set and determined, but the corners of her mouth have begun to relax a little.

"You going to take applications for the job?"

"I don't think so. There's only one person I know well enough to trust my life to. Are you interested?"

"Maybe." I study her eyes, which look into mine with a cool detachment. "I've got a question."

Gaby nods. "Only one?"

"For now. How did you know I wasn't allergic to bees?"

Gaby's expression doesn't change. "I didn't," she says. "I took a chance. It's rare; I don't know what the odds are of it happening like that. Once in—" She lifts her hands.

"In a blue moon?"

"Something like that." Gaby smiles.

247